MW00761790

Ballet Busters
Leap into the
First Nutcracker

Marti

Julie

Luis

Zack

Miss Sophia

Willow

Nancy

Denise

Tasha

Ballet Busters Leap into the First Nutcracker

FIRST IN THE DANCING DOORWAYS SERIES BY
Debra DeVoe

ILLUSTRATED BY
Karel Hayes

Dancing Doorways Academy

A Chapter Book

text copyright@2020 by Debra DeVoe

illustration copyright@2017 by Karel Hayes

Dancing Doorways Academy
Debra DeVoe

www.dancing-doorways.com
dancingdoorways@gmail.com

ISBN: 978-1986531023

This is dedicated to my first ballet teacher, Bernadine DeMike, artistic director of the Royale Dance Theatre, who instilled the love of ballet in all her students. It is also dedicated to my mother, Jeane Evans, who sewed tutus and drove me to my ballet lessons.

Gratitude

First, hats off to my many teachers, among them Bernadine DeMike of Royale Dance Theatre, Yurek Lazowski of the Ballet Russe, Scott Ray of State University of New York at Geneseo, Maida Withers of George Washington University, and SaliAnn Kriegsman, who inspired me to research and write about dance.

A nod to my childhood dancer friend, former associate professor of dance education at Towson University, Sandra M. Perez, for her encouragement and her ongoing passion to educate children and future teachers.

Cheers to my dance buddy Carolyn Kelemen for pushing me and proofreading many versions of this book, to my writer friend Aldema Ridge for supporting and encouraging me, and to my dear friend, Katharina Boser for sharing her technical expertise and insights.

Kudos to my performing arts colleagues at Glenelg Country School (GCS). Our adventure to the Fringe Festival in Edinburgh, Scotland, with the teenage *Aesops Foibles* cast taught me anything is possible. A special point of the toe to Tom French for telling me I could write this book and Carole Lehan for saying dreams come true, if you just "tell the story." And a bow of gratitude to GCS's Head of School Greg Ventre for supporting my venture to Russia.

A tip of the hat to my former student, Michele Kelemen, who brings her best to National Public Radio, GCS librarian Angela J. Horjus for perusing and promoting this book, and Suzanne Stone for photography.

A flick of the wrist to the artistic directors of L'Etoile, the Russian Ballet Academy of Maryland, Svetlana Kravtsova, and Vadim Pijicov for making possible my glorious visit to the Vaganova Ballet Academy in St. Petersburg.

Outstretched arms of appreciation go to my illustrator Karel Hayes and editor and designer Margaret Rose Caro for inspiring me and keeping me focused. And a wave of the hand to Lois Szymanski for her editing and encouraging comments.

Finally, a wink of the eye with love to my mother Jeane Evans and my sister Karen Evans, for believing in me.

Table of Contents

⇨

1
Leap!

I heard the rumble as soon as I jumped out of the car. Something was wrong. I was at Dancing Doorways Academy all right. Twinkling lights sparkled around the flashy sign outside, showing they were open, but there was something different going on. The red bricks almost shivered, as if a mini-volcano inside was starting to erupt.

I waved *adios* to my family, while a red pick-up truck whizzed up to the curb. My buddy Zack gave his dad a quick hug and popped out of the front seat. After speaking Japanese to his father, they both laughed. He slammed the door, and the truck pulled away. Zack turned and looked up at puffs of gray smoke floating from of the top of the building.

"Oh wow, Marti!" he exclaimed and pushed his straight black bangs out of his eyes. "That's coming out right above the stage."

"We'd better get inside," I said. "I don't want to be late for our big trip. I've never been to Russia."

Brakes squealed and another car skidded to a stop behind us. "Hold up a minute! Wait for me!" We stopped on the steps and looked down.

"Okay, Luis, but hurry up," said Zack. "We can't miss The Ballet Buster Super Time Tunnel!"

"The building sounds like a small factory," said Luis. "First *Nutcracker* ballet, here we come. Let's see what's going on."

We pushed the doors open. Inside, it was a madhouse. Dancers from Dancing Doorways Academy ran around like crazy.

"There it is!" I pointed to a gigantic brown trunk with black leather straps. It sat on the stage, shaking with a dull rumbling sound. "We better begin packing."

As I threw my ballet clothes into the trunk,

I heard a low buzz. The sound was hidden deep inside. The huge tower shook, like a helicopter ready to take off. I tossed in my toothbrush and some raisins in case I hated Russian food.

Whoops! Of all things, I almost tripped over the untied ribbons of my ballet slippers. I will tell you more about when I was little, but right now…

Tap, tap, tap. Oh, Zack just tapped me on the shoulder. I let out a breath. "Now what?"

"Hey Marti, I just tossed my jeans and soccer ball into that trunk over there. I also threw in my pajamas. Don't forget yours."

My pajamas? Oh no. I just remembered. A soccer ball? It is winter and snowy in Russia.

Swish, swish, swish. I slid over to the trap door in the middle of the stage, the one that covered the time tunnel. Clanging sounds came from below the stage. My untied ribbons dragged along, so my feet slipped out of their shoes. The wooden floor, worn and rough from many shows, caught my tights and made a run up the side.

"Marti," sighed Miss Sophia. "For the tenth

time, knot your ballet slippers or you'll trip into the Ballet Buster Super Time Tunnel and get lost." She nodded her head three times. Miss Sophia always nodded her head when something was important.

"Okay," I mumbled. I tied my ribbons again and prepared to jump into the black tunnel in the middle of the stage.

The only adult to time travel with us is my ballet teacher, the one and only, Miss Wusslepoof.

"Come here, dancers," Miss Sophia said.

We shuffled to the stage. The trap door was still closed.

"We need to gather around. It's almost time for our trip."

The velvet green stage curtains were old and musty. My nose crinkled from their bad soft cheese odor.

"Wait a minute," said Miss Sophia. She pointed at us again. "Zack, Marti, Julie, Luis, Denise, and Nancy...There should be seven Ballet Buster dancers. Who's missing?" Her turquoise eyes opened wide. "Where's Willow?"

Oh my, Willow was late. Rather, her mother was late. Willow always showed up to our ballet classes after they had started. On top of that, Willow was new to Dancing Doorways. She seemed okay, but I did not know her that well.

"We can't wait much longer for Willow," said Miss Sophia. "Marti, you're on. It's your job to open the trap door."

And ta da! This was my big moment. My arms shook when I slowly yanked the solid wooden trap door.

Thud! It slammed, opening on the stage floor. Out whiffed a puff of gray fog.

"Marti, what's down there?" asked Zack. His shiny black bangs almost covered his eyes. "I can't believe it goes through the center of the earth."

I peered into the nothingness. It was like a night sky without the moon. I felt a tingle in the air.

"It's dark. Like a hole going nowhere," I said.

"I don't want to go 'nowhere,'" said Julie. She shook her head. Her light blue eyes looked scared. Julie is my Best Friend Forever, my BFF. She had to go with us.

17

I pointed to the hole. "Julie, that's where we have to leap. It's not scary. It's exciting."

"It may be very scary, but this large black hole will take us where we need to go," said Miss Sophia. "Ballet Busters, we'll blast back over 125 years, to learn about the first *Nutcracker* ballet. I can't wait for you to take their ballet classes. You'll stay in little rooms with fireplaces, the only heat source. There are no cars. Instead, we'll see horse and buggies. Julie, if you're lucky, you'll see Russia's czar. He went to the first show."

I always wondered what it felt like to dance *The Nutcracker* when the steps were first taught. What did the dancers think the very first time they heard the music? Did they like the dances? We were all going to find out.

Julie's hand shook while fingering her BFF necklace. She had one half of the gold heart, and I had the other. I reached for my BFF necklace. Wait a minute! It was gone. I must have left it in the dressing room. I could not leave without it. I bolted to back of the stage.

"Marti!" yelled Miss Sophia, "Where are you going? Come back. You'll miss the Time Tunnel!"

"I'll only be a minute," I shouted as I pushed open the dressing room door. "I forgot my necklace."

"Hurry!"

I tossed tights and puffy skirts off the benches. Oh no!

"Marti, do you see Willow there?" Miss Sophia's voice sounded shrill.

I could barely catch my breath. Where was the necklace? How could I have lost it?

"We can't wait much longer!"

I glanced in front of the bright lights of the makeup tables. Nothing.

I heard Julie plead, "Forget it, Marti. Please, just come."

I spied a little pink glittery backpack. I ripped at the zipper and knocked over a water bottle. Splash! Water sprayed over everything. Oh no. I'm in trouble now!

I scrambled to the doorway. On the floor, I saw a glimmer in the light. My golden necklace. Victory! I scooped it up and dashed to the stage.

"Marti, run!" Miss Sophia's hands were flying in the air. "We need to get jumping."

I landed next to Julie and she smiled slightly. My head throbbed, while my heart skipped a beat.

"Did you see Willow?" asked Miss Sophia.

I could not speak. I was out of breath. I shook my head no.

"Oh dear," said Miss Sophia. "Well, we can't waste another second. We might try to get her later." Our teacher's head turned as she gazed into our eyes. "You must all think Russia…1892, the year of the first *Nutcracker*."

We grabbed hands and repeated, over and over, "Russia 1892 … Russia 1892." Miss Sophia pushed the huge Magical Trunk that held all of our goodies to the edge of the hole. It buzzed over us like a brown mama bear. A big sign on the side read:

ST. PETERSBURG OR BUST!

To: Ballet Busters, Imperial Theatre School, Theatre Street. St. Petersburg, Russia, 1892

From: Dancing Doorways Academy, Maryland, United States of America

We watched as Miss Sophia pushed the Magical Trunk over the edge. Flash! It was sucked into the darkness.

"You know the drill," said Miss Sophia. She nodded her head two times. "When I say 'leap,' hang on tight and go! We must do this together."

Oh my, the bees in my tummy hummed away.

"Get ready," said Miss Sophia. "The Ballet Buster Super Time Tunnel is almost ready for us."

"Wait for me," said a voice from far away. It must be poor Willow. But we could not wait.

I squeezed Julie's hand. But something was wrong. Her grip loosened in mine.

"I can't," Julie shrieked. "I'm too scared."

"We have to do this together," I yelled. "Hang on!" I squeezed her fingers.

"Ballet Busters, let's go ... Goodbye Dancing Doorways Academy. Russia, here we come. One, two, three, LEAP!" Miss Sophia said.

I held my breath and pinched my eyes shut. "So long world!"

I yanked Julie's hand. One leg reached into the empty air, and I pushed off with the other. I pulled her in with me. Julie's scream echoed.

My dark brown curls flew up as the wind whooshed past my ears. We dropped into the

Ballet Busters Super Time Tunnel. I could not catch my breath.

I opened my eyes. Colors raced through the blackness ... red, pink, yellow streaks.

Sets and costumes whizzed along the Ballet Busters Super Time Tunnel. Flashes of light zipped past with rays of purples, pinks, and greens. Fluffy white tutus trimmed with gold sparkles floated by. Tiaras glowed against the dark. Pink ribbons from thousands of *pointe* shoes flew this and that way. Wooden nutcrackers painted in red, white, and yellow just missed hitting us. Giant soft shimmering snowflakes grazed our heads.

Zack yelled, "Duck!" A huge glittering sleigh shot past my head.

I felt like I was falling down an elevator shaft. The bees in my tummy were going crazy. Musical chimes from *The Nutcracker* filled my ears.

Just when my arms began to ache from holding on, we arched and landed on a wooden floor. Plop! White flashes burst around us. I opened my eyes and could not believe the sight.

2
Landed!

I blinked. My mouth was so dry I couldn't speak. We were not in Maryland anymore. Six dancers and one teacher sat in a circle. I glanced around the room. We sat in heaps on a rose red rug, like frozen statues.

Flecks of snow floated past the windows. Crackling flames from a fireplace burned my nostrils.

Miss Sophia's chin trembled. "Ballet Busters, we made it!" She tucked strands of hair behind one ear. A silver streak shot through the front of her black hair. "Let's go!"

We slowly stood up on shaky legs.

Zack's eyes opened wide. "Whoa, what happened?" He stared at his legs. "My knees are knocking."

Luis chimed in. "My legs feel like bees are buzzing up and down inside."

My aching body quivered as I tried to unfold it. I felt like I had stepped on dry land after a long journey, floating on a boat. All of us found our "sea legs," except for Julie. Her head curled over. She hugged her knees.

Miss Sophia frowned and bent down next to Julie.

"Honey," she whispered, "we're in Russia and we're okay."

Julie looked up. "Everything feels strange." Her eyes were red, and she wrinkled her eyebrows. "I miss my mom and dad and my dog." She looked around.

Miss Sophia took Julie's hands and gently pulled her to stand. "I know. It will take time for all of us to get used to this new place. Marti, take Julie's hand. I don't want her to feel alone."

"Sadly, the new girl, Willow, missed our Super Time Tunnel." Miss Sophia shook her head and told us, "No crying over spilled milk."

No crying over spilled milk? "What did she mean? I didn't get it."

"Too late to cry after it's already a big mess," Zack whispered in my ear. "Time to clean it up."

"Oh now I know," I said. "We need to stop worrying about Willow and get going."

"I need to check out our Magic Box," Miss Sophia said.

I could not believe my eyes. On a plain wooden desk sat a huge glittering golden box. A candle glowed over the sparkling jewels on top. Streaks of color burst across the room.

"Well, it's about time," a voice piped up. "I've been dying to see what's in the Magic Box."

What a disrespectful thing to say. I looked over. Yes, it was Mean Girl Denise. She rolled her green eyes and smoothed the top of her tangled brown ponytail.

"You can wait a minute," I said. "It isn't all about you. Miss Sophia has to take care of Julie first." I softly squeezed my BFF's hand.

"Hey, she's not the only one suffering," said Denise. "I barely made it here alive … all those colors and flying props practically killed me."

Zack and Luis looked at her in disbelief.

"Drama Queen," Zack mumbled.

"We'll have to deal with them," I whispered to Zack and Luis, hoping Denise and sidekick Nancy couldn't hear me.

I glanced at Julie's necklace with the half jagged gold heart and grinned. I reached for my matching half heart necklace with the engraved BFF.

Zack walked to the desk. "Miss Sophia," he said, "you need to come here. Your name is on this fancy box."

"Dancers, we must be nice to each other," said Miss Sophia as she walked over to Zack. "Okay, Ballet Busters, inside are all our secret tools."

We gathered around the huge wooden container decorated with flashy rubies, emeralds, and sapphires. Zack was right. On top in flowery gold letters it read: Mistress Sophia Violet Wusslepoof – PRESS HERE – and an arrow pointed to a blazing star.

Miss Sophia carefully tapped her thumb on the star. Nothing happened.

"Oh no," said Miss Sophia. "It should have popped open." She poked it again. She nodded her head three times. "I'm getting worried. Soon, we'll have to jump in again and go back."

She rubbed her thumb and fingers together, and, after twirling them in the air, rubbed the star in a little circle. This time, the top flew open.

"I just needed the magic touch," said Miss Sophia. "Ballet Busters, are you ready? Let the magic begin!"

Miss Sophia reached inside and lifted out a small silver jeweled box and then gathered a pinch of glitter. She flung open her arms, and tiny silver stars filled the air. Little sparkles settled on top of our heads. We all started chattering in Russian.

How did that happen? Then, we all giggled.

"Now you're Imperial Ballet dancers," she announced with a smile, naming the famous Imperial Theatre School. Imperial meant royal, because the czar's dancers were trained at this school. These children performed in the very first *Nutcracker*.

"Remember, with this magic, you'll blend in. Russian dancers will think we're visitors, of course, but we'll look like we belong to this time period," Miss Sophia said.

She lifted a tan leather pouch out of the jeweled box. Printed on the outside was: BALLET BUSTERS KEYS. She dumped out the keys on the desk. Clang! They hit the wood.

"Here are your room keys." With one big nod of her head, we suddenly had keys in our hands. "Don't you dare lose your key."

My metal key was as long as a pencil, but as heavy as a horseshoe. The metal top had a curlicue flowery design.

"Don't drop it on your foot," said Julie grinning. It was good to see her finally smile.

"Let's get to our rooms, so we can rest."

We followed Miss Sophia into the chilly hallway. She carried a candle to light the way. The odors of burning wood and old musty rugs hung in the air. The wooden steps creaked as we walked up behind Zack and Luis.

Finally, we reached the top floor. There was our Big Brown Mama Bear Trunk.

"Nice," I said. My fingers stroked its sides and I felt some big dents. Those flying wooden nutcrackers and the silver sled must have slammed into it. When I put my ear next to it, no sounds. The buzzing had stopped.

Finally, Julie and I were alone in our bedroom. We ran to look out the window between three tiny beds. We parted lace curtains and pressed our noses to the pane of glass. Long yellow buildings with lots of windows lined Theatre Street. Snowflakes landed on the shiny brick street below. Horses clopped on the stones, pulling carriages with jiggling bells. There were no cars. I felt as if I needed toothpicks to keep my eyes open, I was so tired.

"This is my bed," I said. "We can save the other one for Willow, if she ever gets here."

"Oh no," said Julie, her heart lost somewhere. "I forgot it."

"Forgot what?"

"My photo of Ginger," she said, placing a small frame on the nightstand. "I just have my picture of Mom and Dad, not my dog."

"That's too bad," I said, putting my family photo out so they smiled at me.

"I know Ginger is by the door at home, waiting for me." Julie's voice cracked.

I didn't want her to cry again.

"Julie, I know it's sad, but we'll be back home before you know it. We're both so tired. I need to get some sleep. I'm going to lie down."

Ouch! The straw mattress was scratchy, like little pins in my back. I tugged the striped blue blanket over my ears. And with that, we fell asleep, or as they say in Russian, *coh*.

Thump, thump, thump! Knocking on the door woke me up. I sat upright in bed.

"Enough beauty sleep," said Zack through the bedroom door. "Time to rise and shine."

After a softer knock on the door, a girl entered. She carried wood in her apron. She knelt at the fireplace to add fuel to the fading flames. As quietly as she entered, she left.

"Was that a ghost?" asked Julie.

"I think she was a maid, fueling our fire," I said. "We don't have any heaters."

"This is a strange place," said Julie. "Everything feels so different."

We didn't know it then, but everything was about to get even stranger.

3
Russia

I pushed open the heavy wooden doors of The Imperial Theatre School. Girls with tight braids fastened by big white bows brushed past. Our blue dresses matched the uniforms passing by. Boys clutched leatherbound books and knocked us out of the way. Denise and Nancy squished into the crowd ahead of us. Zack and Luis squeezed upstairs with Julie and me. We raced up two steps at a time.

Bees buzzed in my tummy again. I could not eat the bread and butter at breakfast, so I sipped a glass of warm tea and sugar. I dreamed of Abuelita's rice pudding.

Julie and I entered the large dance studio.

Dull looking mirrors and barres, or poles, lined the walls.

Boom, boom, boom! The ballet master pounded his stick on the floor. Dancers hurried to face the barres. I smoothed my little cotton skirt. My hands quivered as I placed both hands on the long wooden rod in front of me. Julie stood next to me with her feet in a "V," ballet's first position. The Russian girl on the other side, the one with light-brown braids wrapped around her head, glanced at me briefly and then looked straight ahead at the pale blue wall. Whew, I blended in, was one of them.

The wrinkled hand of the ballet master moved up and down as he banged the stick on the floor to keep the beat of the music. The violinist played faster.

The teacher strolled around the room, staring at us. His stick pounded on the wooden flooring as he walked. I pointed my foot and tilted my head to the side. I did not want his stick to hit me. No way. Out of the corner of my eye, I saw him headed towards me. He stopped and rounded Julie's hand.

Whew. Just when I thought I was safe, Whack!

The ballet master tapped my bent knee with his wooden stick. Ouch! My leg stung. It hurt, but I could not rub it. I fought back a tear. What a terrible start! The Russian girl next to me turned to stare at me. Her huge hazel eyes squinted with sympathy. She shrugged and turned to do the next step. Her look made me feel better. I took a breath.

Class was finally over. We walked into the hallway.

"Marti, everything always happens to you," said Julie. She spied Zack. "Hey Zack, you won't believe what happened to Marti!"

Zack and Luis rushed over.

"The guys jump so high here," said Zack. His strong arms reached high above his small body.

"Yeah," said Luis. His curly dark hair was sweaty. "I landed after a leap and looked up, and the Russian boys were still in the air."

Zack saw my frown and asked, "What happened to you?"

"You'll never believe it," I said. "I got hit with his stick, well, brushed with it. The ballet master tapped my knee when it wasn't straight."

"Oh," said Zack. "That must have hurt. Whoops, we're going to be late for our *Nutcracker* rehearsal. Follow me."

We entered a huge studio for the *Nutcracker* practice. Loud voices echoed in the room. Two men argued by the piano. As we tiptoed closer, I remembered seeing one of the men in Miss Sophia's ballet book. Lev Ivanov did some of the dances in the ballet.

Thump! Master Ivanov banged his fist on the piano. His mustache twitched. We froze in place and listened.

"We must move forward," stated the famous ballet master. He pounded his hand on the piano again, and then straightened his tiny eye glasses.

Oh my! Maestro Tchaikovsky, the man who wrote the music, drooped forwards. He sat on the piano bench, clearly unhappy. He wrung his hands, shook his head, and nervously stroked his gray pointy beard.

"We came to Russia at a tough time," whispered Miss Sophia. "Master Petipa started making the steps of *The Nutcracker Ballet*, but he was older and not well, so Master Ivanov took over at the last minute. It was not easy, which is why he pounded on the piano."

"*Da, da,* yes, yes," the composer lifted his long hands and played some notes on the piano.

Master Ivanov turned away from the piano and picked up his stick. He looked out at the swarm of dancers and banged his stick. "My young Imperial Dancers, this is the first practice with the famous Maestro Tchaikovsky. I have taught you the steps with counts, but you have never heard the music. Now we'll have the plea-sure of hearing the music for the first time." He paused and glared at the pianist. "Rather, I hope it will be a pleasure." He pounded his stick into the floor. "Places for Act One!"

The dancers hurried to the sides of the studio. There was a party scene at the very beginning of the ballet. When Miss Sophia told us to sit and watch, I sat between Julie and Zack. The Mean Girls stood in the back.

Zack pointed over at Denise and Nancy. "Look, they're already pointing out the Russian children who are messing up their steps."

Luis sat next to Zack. "Those Mean Girls are at it again. I can't believe it, added Zack."

"I hope the Russians see how awful they are," I added.

Light, quick piano notes twirled in the room. Boys and girls swarmed in toward the imaginary Christmas tree. Many adult men and women whisked around, pretending to hang ornaments on the tree. The children dashed over to the tree and jumped up, trying to reach its top. Clara, the main little girl in the ballet, stood over to the side.

Master Ivanov clapped his hands. "Stop!"

The music paused and everyone froze. The ballet director walked over to the children.

"You're all too stiff. This not an old-fashioned ballet. It is 1892, a new era! You must pretend to be excited about the party. Run, skip, or laugh. The boys can play Leap Frog over each other. Brother Fritz must be a troublemaker. Only Clara stands to the side."

Master Ivanov pointed to the Russian girl at the edge of the space. Her black hair framed a long white face. "Clara is seeing a bright green light beaming offstage. This shows the audience that magic will happen later. Now let's try this again from the beginning."

Another Russian girl in a pale pink net skirt passed in front of us. Her hazel eyes reminded me of someone. Then I remembered!

4
Willow

"That's the girl," I said, touching Julie. "She was the one next to me in class this morning. She had brown braids around her head."

"You're right," said Julie. "She glanced at you when you got tapped by the stick. She was really nice. What's her name, I wonder?"

The girl left us and breezed across the floor, mixing with the other children. Master Ivanov briefly grinned when the children pretended to play.

He clapped once. "Clara, join the circle dance with the other girls. Hug the guests as they arrive."

The boys and girls made two straight lines.

They bowed to each other. The girls turned while the boys clapped. They did sliding steps together and then joined hands to form "London Bridge." Other children ran under all the arms, laughing all the way.

My back began to ache. Julie and I were slowly losing steam. Miss Sophia came over.

"Time to go for supper," said Miss Sophia. "End of a long first day."

Later, I crawled into bed and pulled the heavy scratchy blanket under my chin. Julie was already asleep. The moonlight beamed onto my bedside table. Outside my window, little bells tinkled as sleighs carried people across the icy roads. Horses' hooves pounded on the street.

Wait! Where's the photo of my family? I said "Goodnight" to them every evening. I wanted to turn on a light. Then I remembered there was no electricity. I glanced on the floor. The picture had fallen down.

Yikes. I bent over and whoosh, my elbow knocked the solid huge key from the stand. Clang! It nipped the edge of my big toe. Ouch!

Julie's eyes opened. Her head popped up.

"What was that?"

"Sorry, I dropped the key when I reached for my photo," I said. "Oh, my poor toe!" I rubbed it to stop the pain.

"Well, get some sleep," Julie said. She turned and plopped her head back onto the pillow.

I grabbed the key and placed it gently on the table. I reached down again and picked up the photo. Mama Rosa, with her black hair and dark brown eyes, smiled at me. My head leaned on my mama's arm. My Abuelita had her arm around my other shoulder. My little sister, Francesca, had her curly hair pressed against my mom. We stood in front of the Washington Monument.

I stared at myself. Some people say I look more like my dad with his tan skin. I don't re-member him. He passed away when I was little. My mama, my grandma, and my sister all look alike. Do you know the best part of this photo? All four of us have the same great smile.

"Goodnight. I love and miss you all," I whis-pered, even though they couldn't hear me.

I rubbed my aching toe, put my head down, closed my eyes, and listened to the little bells jingling on the sleighs outside. Soon, they became part of my dreams.

≈ ◟ ≈

Ouch, I stroked my sore big toe. That key really whacked it. On top of that, the audition for *The Nutcracker* was this afternoon. Just when I needed to be at my best to get a great part, my toe hurt.

After our ballet class, I sat on the studio floor. I took off my slippers and rubbed my sore toe. It had stopped stinging. There was a tap on my shoulder. It was my teacher.

"Miss Sophia, what are you doing here?"

"Come quickly Marti. It's an emergency," she whispered, nodding three times. "I have your coat here. Grab your slippers!"

She grabbed my hand. We dashed outside and ran across the frozen stones of the courtyard. I could barely keep up. She flew through the door and up the rickety wooden stairs to her bedroom. Bright embers glowed in her fireplace.

"Whew," she gasped. "We're not too late."

44

"For what?" Bees buzzed in my tummy.

"Not bad news, Marti. It's actually good. Remember Willow missed our trip through the Ballet Buster Super Time Tunnel? Well, we got her a new ticket. She's going to show up any minute. I thought you'd be a good friend for her. She can sleep in the extra bed in your room."

I sighed inside. "Our room isn't that big, Miss Sophia. Julie and I like being by ourselves."

"Yes, but Willow needs a bed, and you have an extra one. Besides, Willow is new to the Dancing Doorways Academy. You can show her around and make her feel like she's one of us. You can share your inner Ballet Buster with her. Plus you are the same age and…"

Whoosh! Boom! Kerplop! A blast of heat shot out, like a huge furnace lighting up. A white blaze blinded me and Miss Sophia, and I fell backwards. Through the colors and sparkles, I saw a girl heaped on the rug. It was Willow.

Miss Sophia slowly stood up and went over to Willow. "There, there honey." She put her hands on Willow's hair and gently lifted her chin. "Welcome to 1892," she said with a smile.

45

"You're in Russia."

Willow opened her dark eyes and rubbed her hands together. "Wow, I made it!"

"How was your trip?" asked Miss Sophia.

"I ducked when huge gift boxes and bows flew by. Dolls and toy horses whizzed this way and that. I knew they were from *The Nutcracker* party," she answered.

"You were right," said Miss Sophia. "Marti is here and she'll help you settle in." I finally stood up.

"Hi," I said, remembering to smile. "You can stay in my room with Julie."

"Good," said Willow, slowly standing up. "Oh, my legs are shaking."

"It'll pass," I said.

Willow pointed to the shimmering golden box on the desk. "What's that?"

"That's what we do next," said Miss Sophia. "This is the Magic Box that will make you Russian."

Miss Sophia stroked her thumb and fingers together, twirled them, and rubbed the blazing star in a little circle. The top popped open. The stones flashed red, green, and blue.

She lifted the silver jeweled box and flung the sparkling stars through the air. "Let the magic begin. Welcome Ballet Buster!"

Twinkles settled on the tiny waves of Willow's brown hair as she said her first Russian words. We laughed.

"Now you're an Imperial Ballet Dancer."

Miss Sophia took the leather pouch and pulled out a fancy heavy metal key.

"Do not lose this, Willow," she said firmly.

"And don't drop it on your foot," I added, laughing and pointing to my toe.

"Oh my, yes," said Miss Sophia. "Willow, you'll blend in, and the dancers will think you're a visitor. But you're only a guest. You cannot touch their things or make friends with them."

"You won't believe it," I told Willow. "The ballet master is so strict. He has a stick and he uses it. But you will learn so much."

"We have no time to lose," said Miss Sophia, as she handed us our coats. "The auditions are beginning. My Ballet Busters, let's get back to the Imperial Theatre School!"

We ran across the stones, barely keeping up with Miss Sophia.

"The auditions?" asked Willow. "What are they? I don't get it."

"Oh," I said between breaths. "Auditions are when you dance for the big person who made up the steps, the choreographer. Then he chooses who is in which dance."

"I don't care which part I get," Willow said.

"I want to get a great part, a big part," I said. "I can't wait to show them that I'm a really good dancer."

5
The Tryout

Thud, thud, tap, tap, tap. The ballet master's stick quickly hit the floor in time to the beat. The audition was in full swing. Master Ivanov and the teachers stared at us from the front of the room. They sat behind a table, whispering to each other and taking notes.

I stood under the curved window with Julie and Willow. We wore our little net skirts. Sunlight beamed over the smooth buns on top of our heads. Heavy pale blue window curtains loomed above the three of us.

Then I saw the Mean Girls across the room. Denise peered at me and then turned to whisper something to Nancy. She raised her eyebrows, all the while tucking loose red curls into her bun. Nancy turned back to face me, crossing her arms, as if to say, "You're going to mess up."

I shook my head and turned away. I'd show them. The Mean Girls were not going to win against me.

When it was my turn, my jumps were high and my footwork fast. I was not as good at turns, but, up to now, there were no turns. At least, not yet. Then my luck began to change. We had to spin across the floor with *chainés* or little whipping turns. Oh no, I was always dizzy after only four turns.

All the children lined up at the corner. We took turns doing steps across the floor to the other corner. Zack and Luis pointed their feet and looked across the room. Their heads whipped around as they spotted or looked at a spot on the wall. That way, they did not get dizzy. Luis and Zack ended strong, with no extra hopping.

Oh my, then it was our turn. Julie and I began our turns across the floor. My hands flapped in front of my body, instead of staying still.

"Nyet, nyet, no, no, Little One," the teacher

yelled at me.

Oh dear!

"Bring your arms closer to your body," said the teacher.

I tried, but no luck. My arms wouldn't stay put. Julie finished her turns and held an *arabesque*, with soft arms in front and her foot pointed behind. Almost perfect. Julie was always almost perfect at everything.

"Lovely!" smiled another ballet master.

I took my pose, the same *arabesque*, but he did not even see me. Willow was next to spin across the floor. Her turns were slower than mine. I worked on my turns at the side of the studio. Oh my, I tried to get my arms closer to my body. My hands were wild butterflies fluttering in front. Just when my arms calmed down, the two Mean Girls showed up, brushing right by me.

"You should get your arms in even closer," Denise sneered.

"I saw your good friend Julie's turns," added Nancy. "They were very nice, but she is so stuck up. She thinks she's so good. She'll be lucky to get the mouse part."

"She's not stuck up," I whispered, "You don't even know her. She works hard."

I turned my back and walked away. "Denise and Nancy were being really mean to you," said Willow behind me. "I heard everything. Are they always like that?"

I stopped. "Yes and that was nothing," I whispered. "Miss Sophia thinks they're okay, but they are bullies. They are mean to good dancers who work hard. They don't like anybody who is better than they are. Sometimes they even try to push into me. They always make it look like it's my fault."

"That's awful," said Willow with a frown. "Try to ignore those Mean Girls. They are jealous busy bodies."

We headed back in line to try the steps again. "You were just doing your best," said Willow.

"I know," I said. "Turns aren't my thing."

Leaps across the floor were next. Good thing, I thought to myself. I was great at leaps. Julie waved for me to get in line next to her.

"Hurry," said Julie. "Let's go."

We stretched out our legs together. Our feet hit the wooden floor at the same time. The beats of the violin flew with us. We hit the last pose together and ran to the side. Denise and Nancy were next, then Willow.

I smiled and brushed sweat off my brow. The ballet masters saw I could fly as high as the Russians, I thought. I should get a great part in *The Nutcracker*.

"Good job," said Willow, running towards us after her leaps. "You nailed those, Marti. You really got a good start by pushing through your front leg."

I stopped to show my friends the secret to high leaps. "I just brush my whole foot on the floor."

All of a sudden, whoosh, my back foot was knocked out from under me. Crash! I fell onto the wooden floor. I turned and saw Denise stumble forward and almost fall. Nancy caught her just in time. Mean Girls!

Willow rushed over and helped me stand up.

"You just stay away from her," said Willow to Denise and Nancy. "I saw it. You tripped her."

"I did not," said Denise, pointing her finger almost into Willow's face. "Marti banged into me. Lucky I didn't fall and break my ankle."

Willow took a step back from Denise. "That's a lie. I saw you trip Marti on purpose."

"No way! Marti is just a klutz." Nancy said.

"You can't talk to my friend like that," said Julie. "You're just jealous because her leaps were so high."

"Yeah, right," said Denise. "She almost fell out there. Her leaps barely got off the ground."

"That's not true!" Willow's dark eyes were blazing. "We need to tell Miss Sophia."

"Oh, don't be a little tattle tale to Miss Sophia," said Nancy. "She won't believe you. She loves us. Let's go, Denise."

Both Mean Girls glared and walked away. Lucky for us the audition was over. We stood in front of the mirror and joined in the *révérence*, or bows, to the teachers, but I was still shaking.

❧

The next evening, Julie and I scrambled up

the steep rickety steps to Miss Sophia's room. Julie carried the candle to light the shadowy hallway. We were finally going to find out our parts in *The Nutcracker*. We pushed our way into the room, and Julie placed the candle on the mantle above the fireplace. Then we both sat down on the rug.

I whispered into Julie's ear, "I know I'm going to get a really big part. I've been working so hard and my feet are pointing better than ever."

Julie's mouth closed in a straight line. Then she frowned. "Marti, I don't really care what I part I have. I just want to be a Ballet Buster in Russia and learn all I can."

Oh my. I shrugged. Even though Julie was my best friend, sometimes she's too perfect. I felt a bit like a louse. We sat down on the red flowered rug.

"Ballet Busters," said Miss Sophia, "this is the moment you've been waiting for all day."

She reached into her pocket and pulled out a piece of thick stained paper. She carefully opened the envelope and glanced at the list. Her mouth formed a surprised "O," and her head bobbed four times as she gazed at us from side to side.

"I have some incredible news. You have received better parts in the ballet than we thought. All your hard work has paid off."

I knew it. I could not wait for my name to be called. I would have the role of my lifetime!

6
Bad Luck

Let me begin at the top of this cast list," said Miss Sophia. She squinted at the old paper. "Zack is a Tin Soldier. Denise is a Flower. Nancy is a Snowflake."

I gasped. I didn't think Nancy was good enough to be a Snowflake.

"Luis is a Candy Cane."

Zack elbowed me. "I knew Luis would get a great part. He's a great jumper, and he'll have to hop over hoops."

Miss Sophia stared at Zack. "Please save your comments for later."

Zack looked at Miss Sophia like he had broken her favorite teapot. "Sorry Miss Sophia."

She continued reading the list. "Willow is an Angel. Marti is a Mouse, and last but not least, Julie…"

Miss Sophia continued speaking, but her words sounded fuzzy. It was like she was talking into a thick woolen rug. Me, only a mouse? Really? I would scurry around the stage in a silly thick brown outfit. And, with a mouse costume head on, so no one would know it was me.

I got the worst part ever. My eyes started to water. I gulped back tears and bit the inside of my mouth. My tummy felt like the butterflies were stuck in a clump. I came all this way for this silly part?

"I don't believe it!" exclaimed Julie. I was jolted by her laugh. Julie's hands were on either side of her huge grin. "This is the best day ever. A Party Guest!"

Julie turned and grabbed my elbow. "Marti, I carry a gift, and I get to play with the nutcracker, and I rock a baby doll, and…"

"You did it," said Zack as he stood up. "You must have knocked those Russians out of the park, Julie!"

"And you're a Tin Soldier," she said. "Good for you, Zack!"

Luckily, they were so excited about their great parts no one noticed me. Julie took the candle and almost skipped out of the room. I slowly stood up and headed to the door.

Then I heard my name. Uh oh.

"Marti?" It was Miss Sophia. She was the last person I wanted to see now. "Come here."

I brushed my arm across my eyes. I hoped she would not see my tears.

"What's wrong?" asked Miss Sophia. "Are you feeling okay?"

I saw she cared, but I wanted to be alone. I shrugged.

"Marti, is it because you're a mouse? Not every part in a ballet can be big."

I looked down. If I opened my mouth, I might sob. My Abuelita would want me to be a Ballet Buster and be strong. My grandma's words echoed in my head. "Life's not always fair, my little Princess. You must make the best of things."

"You got this part because you're a strong dancer," said Miss Sophia. "It takes a lot of zip to move around the stage fast and miss the soldiers. You'll be with Zack. He's a Tin Soldier."

She reached in her pocket and pulled out a soft cotton handkerchief with lacy pink flowers on it. "Here Marti. Dry your tears. You're a hard worker. Hang in there, and you never know. Sometimes an extra part appears. You might get lucky."

I knew she was right, but I needed some time alone. I needed to lie in my bed, under the warm covers.

She touched my shoulder. "Have a good sleep. I'm here if you need me."

I shrugged and walked out the door.

⚬

The next days were filled with ballet classes, then rehearsals. In the big ballet rooms, we learned our steps and practiced them so we knew them really well. Finally, we began to rehearse our dances on the huge stage.

I watched *The Nutcracker* from offstage, to the side. The mice were in only one scene, so I had a lot of time to see the ballet. The first scene was the living room in Clara's home. Besides having a big Christmas tree in the center at the back of the stage, there was a huge grandfather clock at one side. A dark wooden owl with yellow eyes sat on the very top of the clock.

Lucky for Julie. She was onstage the whole first part. She was a pretend daughter of one of the adult party guests. There were other children party guests, but they were all Russians. The nice Russian girl with the brown braids, was also a child party guest. Julie said her name was Tasha.

The families arrived at Clara's for the party. Julie and Tasha skipped onstage with their pretend parents. Carrying presents to give to Clara and her parents, they bowed and gave a hug.

The children danced in two straight lines to a little marching tune. The boys clapped while the girls spun around. I smiled when Julie ran under the clasped hands for London Bridge.

The music became louder and grand. Clara's grandparents teetered out, bringing more gifts. Julie and Tasha both received baby dolls, so they sat and rocked their dolls. The girl Clara, star of the ballet, had a brother named Fritz. The grandparents gave him a drum with a soldier's hat.

Suddenly, the music got spooky and the lights dimmed. The owl waved its wings. A mysterious older man with a black eye patch and flowing dark cape arrived with huge boxes. It was Herr Drosselmeyer, a magician, toymaker, and Clara and Fritz's godfather.

Pop! Scarves suddenly flew out of Herr Drosselmeyer's sleeve. The magic began.

Out of the boxes appeared mechanical, life-size boy and girl dolls. They danced, stiffly beating their legs and blowing kisses. Julie and Tasha sat onstage and bent their arms like the dolls.

Next came the soldier doll in a tall black hat with a red plume. He beat his flexed feet in the air and pretended to shoot.

This was when I saw it. Julie smiled at Tasha, who was sitting next to her. They both looked like they knew a secret joke. It was a "special friends" look. I felt so jealous my blood turned pea green.

This green blood boiling inside my body,

made me feel unlucky, like I had been cheated out of my dream to have a big part in the ballet. Now, I was losing my BFF Julie to a pretty Russian dancer. How much worse could things get?

7
More Bad Luck

I stood in the dark backstage and watched the party guests leave the stage. The children exited right past me. I turned sideways. Julie whispered something in Tasha's ear. They both looked at each other and laughed. The Russian girl walked away and Julie waved goodbye.

Miss Sophia said we were not supposed to talk to any of the Russian students. We were not supposed to share secrets and laugh with them—or take things from them, even small presents. We were Ballet Busters. After *The Nutcracker* was performed, we would jump back into the Ballet Busters Super Time Tunnel and go home. We were not a part of the first *Nutcracker* story.

We were just there to learn about it.

Julie saw me. "Marti, there you are!"

She walked over, and I realized I was always waiting for Julie. We were supposed to be BFFs. I let out a breath and glared at her.

"That was Tasha. She is our age, and her real name is Natasha. Her father performed with the company when he was younger. She lives in a little apartment with her mother and…"

Julie suddenly stopped and looked at me.

"What's wrong, Marti?"

"You know what's wrong," I said.

"No I don't," said Julie. "How could I know what's wrong?"

"You can't tell?" I asked. "I have a silly mouse part. I'm watching you in your big party scene. I stand all alone backstage. Then you just ignore me for that Russian dancer, Tasha."

Julie's eyes looked small and sad, as if her dog Ginger had been hurt.

"Marti, I'm trying my best," began Julie. "I still miss my family. I'm onstage all alone for such long rehearsals. I finally found a new friend. Tasha looks at me and makes me feel like I belong.

You make friends everywhere," she said, and threw up her hands. "It's harder for me."

"You're forgetting one thing," I said. "One important thing."

Julie's eyes rounded and her hands stopped moving. She froze.

"Oh, you mean what Miss Sophia said. That we can't meet any Russians. That we are of our own time. That Ballet Busters need to blend in."

"Yes, we need to stick to ourselves," I said. "Ballet Busters take care of each other." But deep down I felt Julie liked Tasha better than me. It made me feel yucky. Like my insides were ugly, like pea soup.

Julie's chin dropped. She looked like a marionette with clipped strings.

"I know," she whispered. "I can't help myself. Tasha is next to me in the party scene. We do the same steps. She smiled at me first. Miss Sophia can say what she wants, but I'm out on that huge stage by myself…"

"No you're not by yourself," I said, speaking louder. "The stage is filled with dancers."

"But Marti," Julie's voice also began to rise. "I

am the only one from the twenty-first century. It's scary. I feel so alone."

I shook my head.

Julie looked at me. Her frown made her light brown eyebrows touch.

"Pssst, girls, keep your voices down."

I turned. Willow was behind us. Yikes, I wondered what she had heard. Julie and I hardly ever fight. I let out a breath.

"Oh, hi Willow," said Julie. She shrugged. "We're through talking. I have to be back on-stage."

Tasha whisked by and grabbed Julie's hand. They walked out into the bright stage lights. Willow moved closer to me. "What was that all about?" asked Willow.

I shook my head. "Oh, Julie has made friends with that Russian girl, Tasha. But we're Ballet Busters and aren't supposed to be friends with the Russians, and …"

Willow interrupted, "That's all true, but she doesn't sound like she's being nice to you. You've been a best friend to her. You'd think she'd be nicer."

"Yeah, I know," I said.

I did not feel like talking to Willow or anyone else. I needed to be alone, so I made up an excuse. "Willow, I need to watch this next scene. The mice are on after this."

"Okay," she said. "See you in a bit." She left.

I knew Julie felt all alone, but I really did not care. And, deep down, I wanted her part. Julie's photo could end up in dance history books. Her face would shine in the party scene pictures. She could be famous forever. That was my dream.

As I watched the stage, it was Herr Drosselmeyer's turn to pass out gifts. First he pulled out a toy horse. Clara took it, but her brother, Fritz, yanked it away and claimed it for himself.

But then Drosselmeyer reached into his black jacket and brought out the most magical gift, the nutcracker. It looked like a little soldier, but with a strong jaw. I laughed as the children gathered around. The music had a light, playful beat as the nutcracker crunched each nut with a cracking sound. But then in a fit of jealousy, Fritz grabbed the nutcracker and smashed it on the ground. Clara's mouth opened in horror.

But Herr Drosselmeyer sent Fritz to his father and tenderly wrapped the nutcracker's broken jaw with a big white handkerchief. He gently gave it back to Clara. She softly cradled it in her arms and rocked it.

I saw Fritz's angry face as he spun the nutcracker and slammed it onto the stage. I knew how he felt. Herr Drosselmeyer gave Fritz a silly ride-on wooden pony for a gift and saved the special nutcracker for Clara. Fritz really wanted the nutcracker, a colorful wooden doll that cracked nuts. So, after Clara received her present, Fritz turned pea green. He grabbed the nutcracker and slammed it repeatedly until it broke.

I felt hurt and jealous, just like Fritz. I didn't get the gift, the big dance part I wanted. Then, Tasha stole my BFF. On top of that, I hated being a mouse.

8
Mouse Mess

The next day, there I was, back in the dark again. I was at the side of the stage, watching the action under the hot lights.

I tugged at my cotton top. It was bunching up again. I missed my stretchy leotard and tights back home. Then I felt that tap on my shoulder. It had to be Zack. Two taps.

I turned. "What now, Zack?" I burst out.

His dark eyes looked down, like a puppy rejected by its owner.

"Gee Marti, you could pretend to be happy to see me."

"Sorry, Zack," I answered. "Again, I'm looking at the party scene. Again, I'm watching Julie and Tasha, smiling and dancing. And I'm just a lowly mouse."

"Come on," he said. "You're a Ballet Buster. Miss Sophia would say there are no small parts, just …"

"… small actors," I finished for him. "For us, small dancers."

"Besides, Julie's your BFF. You should be happy for her."

But I felt the sickly green snake of jealously slowly twisting around me. I had to stop it.

"Yeah, I know," I sighed. "I'll try to be more cheerful."

"This is a great time to watch the stage," said Zack. "The action on the stage gets to be fun."

"Really? How?"

"Check it out," he said. "After the nutcracker is mended and everyone dances some more, a toy bed appears."

As she watched, the music dropped, soft and sleepy.

"See how Herr Drosselmeyer gently puts the nutcracker in the bed and moves it by the tree?" said Zack.

"Oh, and everyone is saying goodbye and hugging each other," I added.

Whoosh! The children brushed past.

"Zack," I pointed out, "Julie and Tasha didn't even look for us. They just ran by. Julie loves her part but never asks me how I'm doing." I added with a shrug, "I'm sick of them."

"Yeah, you have a point," said Zack.

Herr Drosselmeyer says goodnight to Clara's mother and leaves with a swirl of his cape. Next, Clara walked out in her nightgown. She picked up her nutcracker, curled up on the couch, and fell asleep. Her mother came out with a candle, put her shawl over Clara, and walked off. Herr Drosselmeyer tiptoed back onto the stage, took the nutcracker, fixed it, and put it back with Clara.

"I think this is where the magic happens," Zack said.

Herr Drosselmeyer spun around the room, with his black cape flying. The music changed again, becoming more mysterious. Lights flickered. Thunder crashed. Clara woke up and quickly put the nutcracker back in his bed.

The air tingled with excitement. Herr Drosselmeyer climbed up and moved the owl wings above the clock. Clara looked scared and hid behind the window curtain. "Poor Clara," I said, "because now she gets mice and soldiers."

"And the soldiers are ready to go," said Zack. He held up his pretend golden rifle.

I got in line behind the other mice children. Suddenly we ran onstage, turned, and ran offstage. The soldiers marched out and lined up.

Like magic, the tree grew at the back of the stage. The ornaments sparkled as it rose higher and higher. It was made of cloth but looked real from the front. Clara watched the tree and knelt by her nutcracker. The small bed was pulled off the stage, and a big bed with a real Nutcracker Prince appeared. A mouse ran out, a soldier aimed his fake rifle ... and POP ... the mouse jumped and ran off.

It was our turn. We ran across the stage again. The soldiers saluted and knelt to shoot their gold rifles. We ran out again and stopped in lines. The cannons shot out cheese.

I slid and jumped. It was hard because this

grand stage was raked, meaning it sloped upward at the back. Leaps that moved forward, or downstage, looked higher. Lots of older stages in Europe were like this. My runs and quick jumps felt like I was running straight up hill.

My feet moved like crazy. I got my steps wrong again and again. I never ran the right way. Whack! I always bumped into the same tin soldier. He was a tall Russian boy with curly white hair. He frowned as he pushed me away. My shoulder was sore from where I bumped into him. I rubbed it. A man yelled out, "Cut! Stop! Take a break for ten minutes."

I walked across the stage and headed toward the side of the stage. The bright stage lights blinded me. I held up my hand to shield my eyes.

That is when I spotted it. A light pink ballet slipper with tangled satin ribbons was just off the side of the stage. I picked it up. It had very fine stitching through the leather. It had to be Russian, but where was its owner? I looked around. I even glanced at the feet of the dancers passing by me. They had slippers on both feet.

"Marti!" Zack yelled.

His poke hurt my sore shoulder. "Ouch, that hurts."

"Huh? Oh, sorry, I didn't know."

Not thinking, I tossed the lost ballet slipper in my bag. "It's okay. I'm just so sick of being a mouse. I can't even figure out where to go on the stage. I just scoot and crash into the same soldier."

"Yeah, I was watching you," he said. "I'm lucky. I'll be one of the tin soldiers who live. I'll march off at the end," he laughed. "You'll crash and die."

"Zack, please don't laugh. Not now."

"Okay, this rehearsal is over. Let's hurry back to our rooms. Miss Sophia has something important to tell us."

We dragged up the flights of wooden stairs.

"Have a seat on the rug," said Miss Sophia, as we entered. Zack and I squeezed next to Willow.

"There's something some of you are forgetting," Miss Sophia said, looking at us.

Uh oh. Miss Sophia nodded her head five times. This was not going to be fun.

"What's the rule about Ballet Busters making

friends with the Russians?"

Hands shot into the air. "Okay Zack, fill in your friends."

"We can't make friends with the Russian dancers. We can smile and say nice things if they talk to us first. But that's all. We're not a part of their world."

"That's correct, Zack," said Miss Sophia. "I liked that way you said that. And what about touching or taking things belonging to the Russian students?"

"We can't," said Nancy. "We can't take anything back with us through the Ballet Buster Super Time Tunnel."

Miss Sophia added, "We can only take back what we brought." Denise raised her hand. "Yes, Denise?"

"I saw someone steal a ballet slipper after rehearsal today," she said. "I don't want to be a tattletale, but …" Denise's eyes squinted and looked at me. My ears get hot. My hand went into my ballet bag, and I felt the pink slipper. I had forgotten about it. My stomach flip-flopped.

Miss Sophia's mouth dropped as she turned

to me. "Marti? You?"

Yikes! My cheeks must have been as red as a firetruck. I reached in my bag and gingerly pulled out a slipper. The dancers gasped.

"I … I'm so sorry, I didn't mean …" My voice was little and weak. Zack saved me by grabbing the slipper and handing it to Miss Sophia.

"I'm surprised at you, Marti," she said, with piercing eyes.

"I don't think she meant to keep this," said Zack. He glared at Denise. She sweetly smiled back. I could not believe it!

"Marti, I need to talk to you," said Miss Sophia. "Everyone else, go clean up for supper."

"I know you didn't do it on purpose," whispered Julie. "Good luck, Marti."

I wanted to be anywhere else. Even a mouse crashing into mad soldiers would be better than this. Miss Sophia looked at the slipper and smoothed out the wrinkles in the pink ribbons.

"Well?" She looked right at me.

"I didn't mean to take this. I just saw it backstage and picked it up. Right when I was going to tell someone, Zack came and touched my sore shoulder. It ended up in my ballet bag by accident."

"Marti, you know we need to blend in so we can learn about *The Nutcracker*. A Russian girl is missing her slipper and it's a Ballet Buster's fault."

I dropped my head into my hands. "Sorry, I'll be more careful."

"Okay Marti, I don't want to send anyone home early through the Ballet Buster Super Time Tunnel. I'll make sure this gets back to the right dancer. Go."

Whew! I went back to our room. On the way, I stopped at the sink and splashed cold water on my cheeks to cool them down. I looked at my face in the scratchy old mirror. My Abuelita would not be happy with me. But she would be glad I apologized.

ﻋﻠﻰ

After dinner, Zack, Willow, and I walked back to our rooms. Out in the dimly lit hallway, Luis came over.

"Hi Guys," said Luis. Then he looked at me. "Um Marti, I'm surprised you stole that ballet slipper."

I started to open my mouth to say something, but Zack jumped in. "It was an accident. I saw it. You didn't even know you were doing it, right Marti?"

"Yeah," I said. "I don't want to talk about it anymore."

Zack changed the topic. "Hey Luis, what happens in the ballet when the soldiers and mice fight?" he asked.

Luis scratched his scalp of curly dark brown hair and smiled.

"Come on, fill us in. We need to know what happens."

"Come over here," said Luis, "so we don't bother the others." He leaned against the window sill. It was already dark outside.

"Yeah," said Willow, "What happens next? The dancers didn't get through all of it today."

I let out my breath. "That's because I kept goofing up as a mouse."

"Well," said Luis, as he looked at me. "It's easy

to get mixed up. A lot can happen in a short time," he grinned. "After the cannons shoot out cheese, Clara wakes up the nutcracker in his bed. Mice are being shot right and left. After they fall, they're dragged off the stage,"

"That's what happens to me as a mouse," I said. "I don't live."

Luis continued, "The Mouse King leaps out with seven heads. He is really scary looking. He fights the nutcracker. Just when it looks like there's no hope, Clara throws her shoe and hits him on the head."

Zack poked me. "Hey Marti, maybe that's the slipper you took." He grinned.

"Not funny," I replied.

Luis brought us back to the story. "The Mouse King runs over to get Clara, but when he does that, the nutcracker takes his golden sword and stabs the Mouse King in the back."

"Whoa!" said Zack. "I heard the Mouse King dies, and the nutcracker slices off his crown with a golden sword."

"The mice pick up their king and carry him off," said Willow. "The mice pretend to cry as the

Mouse King goes off."

"Then the music changes," I added. "Harp sounds float through the air."

A glow of candlelight grew on the hallway wall. It was Miss Sophia.

"And Clara falls asleep in her bed," said Miss Sophia, walking closer. "And it's time you all returned to your rooms. Sweet dreams, Ballet Busters."

I scooted up the stairs with Willow. I didn't want to get into anymore trouble with Miss Sophia.

9
Mean Girls

Willow stood next to me as we watched in the wings at the side of the stage. This was the start of the Snowflakes rehearsal. Clara's bed flew out the window while she slept in it. Delicate music played, creating an air of excitement. The bed traveled over the tops of villages. Finally, it landed in a snow forest and spun in circles.

The nutcracker appeared. In a blink, his soldier costume changed and he became a Nutcracker Prince. He took her hand, with a kiss. The Nutcracker Prince put a crown on Clara's head, and they walked offstage together.

The back of the stage had a huge backdrop of

big pine trees covered with snow. It looked like white puffy blankets covering the prickly green needles. The Snowflake dancers were waiting on both sides to go on and perform.

Oh no! Just our bad luck. The Mean Girls were back. I forgot Nancy was a Snowflake! Denise stood next to her and helped Nancy with the headpiece in her hair.

Nancy wore a huge headband with little white puffballs on wires. These balls floated above her head. "Ouch, it's poking my ear," said Nancy, rubbing the spot.

I turned and looked. Denise reached over and tucked in a wire, pushing against the layers of her white gauze skirt.

"Be careful!" said Nancy. "Don't crush my skirt."

"Hey, I'm only trying to help here," said Denise. "Be nice."

The little puffballs on the dancers' heads glowed in the dark. A couple feet away, Julie and Tasha practiced their dance with the baby dolls.

Nancy looked over at Julie and Tasha with their babies and turned to Denise. "I'm so tired of seeing them rock their dolls," said Nancy, with an eye roll. She looked over to us, making sure we overheard. "Julie has this perfect little curtsy at the end of her dance. It's enough to make me sick."

Denise looked at Nancy and then stared at me. "Look at how Julie smiles at that Russian dancer with the braids," said Denise. "The pretty one, you know who I mean."

"Tasha," answered Nancy. "Yes, she's the only one of them, the Russians, who even looks at us."

"But she only talks to boring Julie," Denise said.

I knew I should stand up for Julie and say she wasn't boring. But the snake of jealousy twisted tighter around me.

Willow spoke up for Julie. "She's still our friend. She's working hard on her dances in the party scene."

Nancy answered. "Oh Willow, don't be so sure. I thought your good buddy Marti and Julie were BFFs, or something like that." She pointed her finger at me. "Now they're never together."

All right, I needed to say what was on my

mind. I stepped closer to them. "What?" I asked. "How would you know about Julie and me? We still have our BFF necklaces."

"Yeah, sure. What is it with you and Julie?" said Nancy. The Mean Girls looked at each other, and then glared back at me. "We never see you together anymore."

I gulped. They were right. Julie was never with me anymore. She never had time for her true BFF.

The Mean Girls crossed their arms. They were like two cats waiting to attack. Their eyes flashed in the darkness of backstage.

"Well, you're wrong, both of you," I said. "Julie and I are still BFFs." My voice sounded empty, as if I were talking into a huge seashell.

"You could have fooled us," said Denise with a sly smile. Her head tilted toward Nancy. They both snickered.

Julie and Tasha walked to the prop table, to pick up their baby dolls from their special places marked on the table.

Julie rocked her doll and watched the action onstage. Tap, tap! I lightly poked Julie on her back. She moved away, as both girls put their dolls on the table. Julie whispered something in Tasha's ear. Both of them giggled and shuffled out the side door together.

My shoulders slumped down, like a puppy's tail when no one petted it. I knew Julie couldn't see me in the darkness, but she didn't care about me anymore.

Willow saw what happened, and it seemed she could read my mind. "Julie just didn't see you," she said. She gently touched my shoulder. "Let's go to the dressing room and get changed."

I shrugged. "You go ahead. I'll catch up."

"Okay," said Willow. "See you there." Willow walked out the door, but I couldn't move.

The worst part was Denise and Nancy saw Julie walk past me and laugh with Tasha. They knew Julie snubbed me.

Denise spoke in a sickeningly sweet voice. "Nancy, did you see that? Julie just ignored her best friend. She knew Marti was watching, but she chose to be with that Russian, that 'what's her name.'"

"Tasha," Nancy said in a singsong tone.

"Oh yes, Tasha. Julie wanted to be with her new Russian BFF instead."

Ouch. That stung. But they were right.

The lights dimmed and then brightened.

Nancy said, "I have to line up for my dance." She got in line behind three other Snowflakes. "See you, Denise!" The music began, and Nancy ran out and leaped across the stage.

I stared at the sea of shaking pom poms. The white puffballs shook above their heads as they turned. Instead of laughing at this silly sight, I felt homesick. I wanted to go home. Nothing on this Ballet Buster adventure was fun anymore. I had a silly mouse part, Julie wasn't talking to me, and now she had a new Russian BFF.

I ached for my family. I needed my Abuelita to hug me. I could almost feel her arms around me and hear her saying, "Princess, life isn't fair. Make the best of it."

I walked over to the prop table. I wasn't supposed to stand there, but I didn't care. I wanted a closer look at the baby dolls. I leaned against the table. It was dark, and I was alone. Then I did the worst thing.

10
Julie's Baby Doll

I don't know why I did it. It was so wrong of me. I stood at the prop table and picked up Julie's baby doll. We were never supposed to touch anything on the prop table. Ever. I hugged the doll and I swayed back and forth on my tip toes. I heard children singing. I danced a couple steps with the baby.

The Snowflakes came out again, and this time they held puffballs on wires with their hands. They crisscrossed with tiny weaving steps called *bourrées*. As the Snowflakes posed, Clara and the Nutcracker Prince walked to the center of the stage. Then they turned and moved upstage to the back, toward the moon and star. Little bits of white paper flickered to the floor when the Snowflakes ran off the stage, through the fake snow. The curtain closed. It was the end of Act I.

As I snuggled with her doll, I felt closer to Julie. Then it all went wrong. Out of the darkness, I felt eyes on me. I froze.

"What are you doing?" Denise hissed. My heart raced. I tried to talk, but nothing came out. I hugged the doll in my arms.

Nancy raced to stand next to Denise. "You're stealing that doll," she said.

I shook my head.

Then, out of the shadows, a stagehand yelled and headed toward me. He lifted his hand. "Freeze!"

"We're out of here!" Denise muttered. She grabbed Nancy and ran away.

Tossing the baby behind the back curtain, I took off.

The man yelled for me to stop, but I kept going. Butterflies in my tummy jumped. I ran into the dressing room, trying to catch my breath. I realized, with the baby doll missing from the table, Julie would be blamed. What a mess!

The door opened. "There you are, Marti. I was looking for you. I was just putting on my BFF necklace and thinking of you."

Oh my goodness. It was Julie. She was the last person I wanted to see. She didn't even know her doll was missing from the prop table.

My face turned red and felt hot. I sat on the floor and took off my ballet slippers, my back to Julie, so she couldn't see my face. I wanted to sink into the floor and disappear.

"Marti!" Julie said louder.

"Just getting ready," I mumbled, feeling like a rat.

"Okay," she said. "I can't wait to tell you about the secret music box. Everyone's talking about it. I'll catch you up back at the room." Julie flew out of the dressing room yelling, "Bye!"

I changed my clothes and walked out, head down. The Mean Girls waited for me in the hall-way, coats on and eyes glaring.

Ignoring them, I headed back to my room to stop the butterflies spinning in my tummy. Before I could get there, Denise stopped me.

"What happened?" she asked. "Did the man

catch you stealing? Did you get in trouble?"

"No," I said. "And I wasn't stealing."

"We saw you take Julie's doll off the prop table. I thought for sure that man got you," Nancy said. "What were you thinking? Why would you ever hold Julie's doll?"

"I don't have to tell you," I said. "You're not my mother."

"Where did you throw the baby?"

I bit my lower lip. "I found it and put the baby back on the table."

A lie. I'd told a lie.

"Well just you wait," said Denise. Her voice sounded low. "Wait until we tell Julie you stole her doll."

11

The Secret Music Box

Please don't tell her," I begged. My heart sank. What a mess.

Nancy squinted her eyes and began to say something, when Zack yelled out, "Marti, there you are!"

"We'll get you later. Just you wait!" whispered Nancy, and then the Mean Girls were gone.

"Whoa, what were they worked up about?" asked Zack. "They looked like they were going to bite your head off."

"Oh nothing," I said. "Just the usual." Another lie.

"Marti, your face is all red," Willow said.

I tried to ignore her.

"We're really tired and heading back to our rooms before supper," said Luis. He pulled a wool cap over his short curls. "Come walk with us."

Outside, fluffy snowflakes whirled around as we crossed the stones. It was dark. We leapt across the icy streets. Horses clopped along, pulling sleighs. Thick woven blankets covered laps of parents as children snuggled in back of the sleighs. Church bells chimed over children's laughter.

Thoughts hurt my head. I could not believe I'd rocked Julie's baby doll and then tossed it in the dark. Why did I touch her doll in the first place? Abuelita would hate all my lies.

Willow nudged me. "Marti, what do you think it is?"

"Huh, what?"

"I knew you weren't listening. What do you think is in Maestro Tchaikovsky's Secret Box?"

I should have been excited about this mystery box, but my life was so upside down because of my bad choices. "I didn't see it. What does it look like?"

"Marti," said Zack. "The box was the big wooden crate in the hallway. It was outside the studios. Everybody was talking about it."

"They say it's the Secret Box of Maestro Tchaikovsky," said Luis. "I thought the box would be little, but it's huge and heavy."

"There are French words on the side," said Willow. "Miss Sophia said it arrived from Paris, France. She thinks it's a new musical instrument."

"I can't wait to hear it," said Zack. "Tasha said Maestro Tchaikovsky might play it for the Sugar Plum Fairy. She's from Italy and rehearses her dance tomorrow."

"Yeah, I can't wait," I said, trying to sound upbeat. But really, I didn't care at all.

That night, I tossed and tossed. My eyes popped open. Why did I touch the doll? Why did Denise and Nancy have to see me? And why, oh why, did I toss the doll behind the curtain and run?

After Denise and Nancy tell Julie, she'll hate me forever. I'll be in so much trouble. Miss Sophia will send me back home, and I'll be a disgrace to the Ballet Busters. Abuelita's face filled my thoughts and tears came.

At breakfast, I pushed the porridge around in the bowl. I picked up my glass and sipped warm tea with sugar.

"Do you feel okay, Marti?" Willow asked.

"I couldn't sleep," I said. "I don't feel like I'm a Ballet Buster anymore."

"Why? What you mean?"

"It's nothing," I said.

"Well, you better get going or we'll be late for class. I'll meet you outside."

Willow and I walked on the snow-covered stones, sliding all the way. Just ahead of us, Julie entered the yellow brick Imperial Theatre School with Zack and Luis. Butterflies clumped together in my stomach.

"Did you ever do something so awful you wished you hadn't?" I asked.

"Yeah," said Willow. "Once I broke my cousin's new toy truck, on purpose, at his birthday party. I was jealous. I wanted the kids to give me presents, too. So I stepped on the firetruck and broke it."

"What happened?"

"Oh, it was a mess. My mother said I had to make it right. I apologized to my cousin while the guests watched. Then I had to earn money to buy him a new truck," she shook her head. "I'll never do it again."

Class sped by quickly. My mind was not on dancing.

After class, I heard tingling sounds in the hallway and peeked in a doorway. All the young dancers were looking down from the balcony into the practice hall below.

I tiptoed to the edge of the black lacy-looking wrought iron balcony. The Sugar Plum Fairy, Antonietta Dell'Era, was lifting her arms, floating across the floor on her toes. Maestro Tchaikovsky played a little piano. The music was light, the notes sparkled in the air.

"That's the secret musical instrument Maestro Tchaikovsky brought from Paris," whispered Julie. "It's called a celesta."

Guilt washed over me. At least Julie didn't seem to know what I'd done. Together, we listened to the "Dance of the Sugar Plum Fairy."

"Let's go back to the room together," Julie suggested. "I'll meet you later by the dressing room door."

Normally I'd be thrilled. But what could I say? "Sure," I said as we parted ways.

A little later, as I left the dressing room, I knew everything had changed. Julie had found out about the missing doll. Miss Sophia hugged her in the hallway and Julie's eyes were red from crying.

Miss Sophia grabbed my arm. "Marti, something awful happened to Julie. Take her back to your room. She can tell you about it. She needs her best friend at a time like this."

When Julie hugged me, I felt like a rat.

"Oh Marti, just the worst thing happened. I'm so glad you're here."

Butterflies jumped in my stomach when Julie took my hand and we began to walk out the door.

"So what happened?" I asked, guilt sliding over me like a coat of slime.

"Marti, my baby doll was stolen. They said I didn't put it back on the prop table after I danced yesterday. But I know I put it back. Tasha saw me put it on the prop table."

"That's awful." I kept my eyes down. I couldn't even look at her.

"Miss Sophia said someone must have knocked it off. Or maybe someone stole it as a mean trick."

She stopped. "If they can't find it, I might be sent back. I'll go through the Ballet Buster Super Time Tunnel all alone." She wiped away a tear. "I don't want to go back, not now. I'm having the best time."

"They'll find it," I said. "They should look on the floor all around the table." My voice sounded weak, like I had a cold.

Then I heard them. The Mean Girls. I couldn't believe it.

"Julie, wait up!" yelled Denise.

"Why should we wait for them?" asked Julie. "Let's keep walking."

We rushed towards the dorm, but they caught up.

"Guess what?" asked Denise, all out of breath.

"Come with me," I begged, looking at Julie. I

tugged her hand. But she stopped.

I felt hot, even though there was ice and snow under my boots.

"We know what happened, and we saw who did it," Denise said.

12
A Rat

D id what?" asked Julie. She frowned at the Mean Girls.

"Stole your baby doll," Nancy said.

"You'll never guess who," added Denise.

"What?" asked Julie. "How could you possibly know?"

"We do know, and you're not going to like it," said Denise. "You're looking right at her."

The Mean Girls stood next to each other with smug smiles.

I felt my face twist in fear.

Denise turned and her finger pointed to me. "Your BFF, Marti!"

I burst into tears, covering my face with

gloved hands.

Julie turned to me. "Marti, you? Is this true?"

I shook my head no, but there were no words. Another lie.

"She stole the doll from the prop table and danced with it," said Nancy. "When the backstage man came, she threw it behind the curtain and ran."

"Like a rat!" said Denise. "We ran, too, before the man got us!" They both laughed.

"Marti," said Julie. She looked at me as if I were a ghost. "Say it's not true. Not my BFF."

"I'm so sorry," I sobbed. "I never meant for this to happen. I didn't steal it. I was missing you. I just hugged the baby and danced a bit. I was going to put it back, but the man came…" My voice drifted off.

"Oh Marti! You lied to me!" said Julie. "My BFF. How could you? All you've done since yesterday is lie to me." She ripped her BFF heart necklace off and threw it at me. "I'll never talk to you again!"

I bent down and picked up half of Julie's golden heart. My tears fell on it. I put the broken necklace in my pocket, hearing her footsteps fade away.

There was a hand on my back.

"Marti, what's wrong?" It was Willow. "Here, wipe your tears." She pulled out a white handkerchief from her bag.

"I've lost everything," I said through my sobs. "My BFF, everything."

"Blow your nose and tell me what happened," said Willow. "We should go inside. Your tears will turn into icicles out here."

Julie wasn't in the room. Willow and I sat on our beds and I told her everything, twisting her cloth handkerchief into a knot.

"I promise I won't do anything like this again, Willow," I said. "I just don't know what to do. I can't undo it. I want to go home."

"You can make it right," she said.

Knock, knock. The door opened and Zack was there.

"Marti, Miss Sophia wants to see you," he said.

I sighed.

"Tell the truth," Willow said.

I slowly walked toward the door.

"I don't know what you did," said Zack with eyes as big as soccer balls, "but it must have been really bad. Miss Sophia can't stop nodding her head."

My stomach turned.

"It's all a big mess," I said.

13
Now What?

I stood for a minute outside Miss Sophia's door. Then I took a breath and knocked.

When Miss Sophia opened the door, her mouth was in a straight line. The gray streak in front of her hair glowed. Julie sat in a turquoise satin chair.

"Marti, I was surprised to hear you stole Julie's baby doll," she said. "Have a seat." Her voice was firm.

The flames in the fireplace lit up the flowered rug. I sat in a wooden chair across the room from Julie. I untwisted the handkerchief and tapped a tear on my cheek. I must not cry...I must not cry. I bit my lower lip. My Abuelita would want me to be brave. She would say I must make things right.

Miss Sophia sat in the chair next to Julie. "Tell us what happened, Marti," she said. "What really happened?"

I gulped. "I saw the doll on the prop table. I knew I wasn't supposed to touch it, but I couldn't help it. I just danced with it a little. Then the big man started to come over."

Miss Sophia said, "Denise and Nancy said you stole the doll."

"No, I never stole it. When the stagehand came, I got scared and threw the doll." I bit my lower lip. I had to say it. "And I ran."

I wiped another tear. Julie stared.

"I was so mixed up," I said. "I haven't had good luck since we got here. I got a crummy mouse part. And then Julie, you were supposed to be my BFF, but you were always with Tasha. I felt so alone."

Miss Sophia nodded her head. "Marti, after you danced with the doll, why didn't you tell the truth? I thought you were a Ballet Buster."

I bit my lip again. "I was so scared," I said.

"Denise and Nancy said I stole the doll. But I didn't. If the man caught me, he would've sent me back home."

"No Marti," said Julie. "They blamed me. If they can't find the doll, I'll go home through the Ballet Buster Super Time Tunnel. By myself."

My tummy flipped. I mouthed a tiny "Oh."

"You're supposed to be my BFF," said Julie.

"Oh Julie," I said. "I'm so sorry. It's all my fault. As soon as I picked up the doll, I knew it was wrong."

"If you knew it was wrong," said Julie, "why did you run and then lie to me?"

I couldn't find the words. I just shrugged.

Finally Miss Sophia said, "Okay, Marti, there must be a way to make things right. Do you know where you threw the doll?"

I looked up. "I think so. Maybe I could look behind the black curtain? If I can't find it, I should go home, not Julie."

"That would be a start. I'll go backstage with you and see if you can find the doll," said Miss Sophia. "There's a lot broken here, but, like the cracked nutcracker, it can be mended. Julie, you can go back to your room. I need to talk to Marti alone."

She hugged Julie before she left. My old BFF never looked at me.

"Marti, we need to decide what's going to happen to you."

Here it comes.

"You seem really sad about all of this. If you didn't care, I would send you back home, through the Ballet Buster Super Time Tunnel. But if you find the baby backstage, you won't have to go home. You've told so many lies," she continued. "I'll need to keep my eyes on you. You say Denise and Nancy are Mean Girls, but you were really mean to Julie."

I bit my lip again. "I know, Miss Sophia. I shouldn't have lied, but I've learned my lesson. I'll make it up to Julie. I promise."

"Come here, Marti." Miss Sophia gave me a hug. At that moment, I felt some of the butterflies in my tummy fly away. Getting the truth out hadn't been easy, but already I felt lighter.

That night I crawled into bed, clutching the photo of my grandmother standing with my family.

"Abuelita," I whispered. "I'm so sorry. Your princess made a mess. I promise you I'll make it right. I need to be a Ballet Buster. I'll make Julie like me again. I'll make it up to her. I want you to be proud of me. Night, night."

I just hoped I could find that doll.

14

Where Is the Doll

The next day, I went backstage with Miss Sophia. We stepped behind the massive velvet curtains.

The toy tin soldiers practiced their moves on the stage. Slash! Whiz! Swords sliced the air.

The stagehand, who had seen me yesterday, came over, frowning. His eyebrows pushed together as he walked us to the prop table. I saw the other props laid out. There were the nutcracker, the gifts, and Tasha's doll. Then there was an empty square for Julie's doll, still missing from the table.

Butterflies hummed again in my stomach.

"I threw it there." I pointed to the side black

velvet curtain. I looked on the ground. Nothing.

Oh please.

The man's arms were bent across his chest.

I looked under the table. No luck. Oh no! I looked behind the curtain. Just empty darkness. "Oh please, let me find Julie's doll," I cried to myself.

Then I turned and saw a flash of pale blue. I bent down and picked up her doll. I wasn't going home!

Miss Sophia smiled. "Marti, one problem solved. Go to the dressing room and change. You have your mouse dress rehearsal. You'll wear your costume today."

༄

We were crammed backstage with other brown furry mice and tin soldiers. My mouse costume felt heavy and bulky. I could hardly move my arms. Willow stood on one side of me. "Well Marti, you look…big."

I rolled my eyes. With the big mouse head on top of me, she couldn't see my eyes roll. She couldn't even see my face.

"Well, I'm out of here," Julie said to Tasha. My tummy sank a little. Would she ever be my friend again?

"I'm staying," said Tasha. "I need to see this. I hope Big Mouse here doesn't get stabbed by a sword." She tapped my side and laughed. I could barely feel it through all the fabric. Not funny.

I felt a poke near my shoulder and turned. I squinted through the holes of my mouse head.

"Over here. It's me, Zack."

"I can't see anything out of this huge mouse head. I almost can't breathe."

"I had a hard time finding you," he said. "You just look like all the other mice. Huge and fuzzy."

I moved my head up and down to try to see him through the holes.

"Your uniform with the tall black hat looks pretty cool," I said. Zack's sword was at his side.

"What? I can't hear you."

I pulled off my mouse head.

"I like your red outfit and black hat," I repeated.

"I'm supposed to be made of gingerbread," said Zack. "You mice are supposed to eat me."

"How can I eat you when I can't see anything

with this head?" I asked.

"Don't worry," Zack answered. "Just follow your lead mouse."

More tin soldiers strutted out holding their swords. They tried to save the nutcracker from the evil Mouse King.

I put on my mouse head and scooted onstage with the pack of mice. Soldiers in straight lines held swords that thrashed everywhere. I kept moving, but could only see blurs of tall black hats and shiny silver.

Yikes! I almost hit a soldier.

I held my furry paws in front and followed the lead mouse. We did a tight little run, whizzing past soldiers and other mice. I moved in line behind the others. Then came the kicks.

Oh no, trouble. I lost my lead mouse. Yikes, where was he? But I kept kicking forward.

Wham! Crash! I bumped into a soldier, and he fell down. I screamed when he yelled, then tripped over him and, boom, was on the ground.

Someone shouted, "Cut, cut!" The music stopped. Uh oh.

15
Oh No!

It felt like I was in a heap of brown fuzz in the middle of everything.

"I'm here, Marti. Hold still." It was Tasha. She gently lifted off my mouse head.

The soldier got up to one knee and rubbed the other. His hat flipped off, showing a mop of blonde hair.

Oh no, not him again. It was that Russian soldier who already acted like he hated me.

"What do you think you were doing?" he yelled. "You've crashed into me before!" He straightened up his back. His tall black boots flashed under the bright lights.

Tasha stood up and broadened her shoulders.

"You should be looking out, too," she scolded to the soldier. "She can't see. Besides, you can't yell at my friend." Then she helped me up.

Master Ivanov hurried over. "What's going on here?" He looked at me through his wire-rimmed spectacles.

My tummy did a flip, and I opened my mouth to speak, but Tasha cut me off.

"Master Ivanov, if I may say something?" she asked.

He looked at her with surprise but didn't reply.

"My dear friend can't see out of her mouse head. She didn't mean to trip over this soldier. It was an accident."

"No, the mouse did it on purpose," blurted the soldier, "and you know it. It's happened before."

Master Ivanov looked at both of us. His fingers stroked his mustache.

"Now, now, Yury," Master Ivanov said to the soldier. "Calm down."

The ballet master looked at my hot, sweaty face and then turned back to the soldier. "I don't see how this little mouse can hurt a big, strong soldier like you."

The soldier lowered his eyes. His ears turned deep red.

"You're right, Master Ivanov. I apologize for being disrespectful and yelling."

The soldier straightened his back, clicked his heels, and said to me, "Mistress Mouse, I'm sorry I yelled at you. I won't do it again."

I couldn't move. Butterflies tumbled in my tummy.

Tasha poked me and whispered, "Say something."

My voice was only a bit louder than a mouse's squeak. "I'm sorry, and I'll try to be more careful."

Master Ivanov snapped his fingers. Click. Click. Click. "Costume Mistress!"

An older woman in a long black dress appeared.

The master pointed at my mouse head. "Fix the eye holes so this poor mouse can see."

The costume mistress did a small bow. The mouse head was whisked out of my arms.

"From the top," said Master Ivanov. We ran

through the scene three more times. I did not trip any more soldiers. I could see mice being stabbed by soldiers with fake swords.

Whish! It was my turn. A phony sword brushed next to my body and I fell on my side. The soldier had "killed" me. A doctor doll grabbed my foot and dragged me along the floor. In the darkness of backstage, I stood up. Tasha and Willow came over, "You did it, Marti."

Zack dashed over. "Let's get out of here before we have to deal with those Mean Girls."

I nodded. "I need to get out of this brown fluff."

"My boots are killing me," said Zack. "I'll come, too." We headed to the dressing room, and then across the square to dinner.

As we dodged shiny little puddles of ice, Zack asked the strangest question.

"What are muffs?"

"What? Fluffs?" asked Willow.

"No, muffs," said Zack. "With an 'M'. Julie and Tasha were talking about them. They said the girls were getting muffs to wear to the festival."

"Oh, I know," I said. "I think a muff is a big roll of fur we put our hands in to keep warm. We wear them instead of mittens."

"Fluffs rhymes with muffs," said Willow. "Muffs are fluffs."

"Yes," I said with a laugh. "We'll be in a huff with fluff on our muffs."

"I think you both must be hungry for supper," said Zack, and he sped ahead.

"But Zack…!" He was already out of ear shot. "Tomorrow Zack will see our muffs."

"I can't wait," said Willow. "The boys are getting new hats for our special adventure."

16
The Russian Fair

The next day I stuck out my tongue to catch snowflakes. Not fake flakes, like in *The Nutcracker.* These were real snowflakes. All the girls stood together near the street. We were going to the Russian Festival. A sleigh, pulled by a horse, would take us there. When Miss Sophia told us, she was excited. Her chin nodded up and down so many times we lost count.

"Hey, so those are muffs," yelled Zack as he walked over with Luis.

Willow waved her muff in the air next to me. "Look at mine with the soft white fur."

"I like your new wool hats," I said, holding

my black fur muff up to my cheek.

"These fur hats are really warm," said Luis.

"There they are!" I yelled. Tasha and her father waved at us from the back of the sleigh.

"Whoa, boy!" The driver pulled back on the reins. The big sleigh stopped in front of us.

"Good evening, everyone," Tasha waved. "Jump in."

Julie pushed me to the side and sat next to Tasha and her father. Willow and I sat with Zack and Luis, across from Julie, Tasha, and her father.

"I would like you all to meet my father," Tasha beamed. "He's a dancer in the Imperial Ballet."

He smiled under his huge fur hat. "Tasha has said so many good things about all of you. It's nice to finally meet you. Put the blanket over your laps. It'll keep you warm."

The horse took off and the sleigh lurched forward. Little bells jingled on the reins as we glided over the icy street. Light glimmered from the sunset. Skaters raced on the frozen Neva River. The horse clopped along the edge of the river and crossed over a bridge. Our faces froze as the chilly wind blew against our noses.

Julie lifted her muff next to Tasha's face and whispered something. I knew it had to be about me, but I wouldn't let Julie ruin my night at the Russian Festival. I would ignore her. I wouldn't even look at her. No matter how I tried to be better, Julie didn't notice.

"What were they practicing today in the *Nut-cracker*?" Tasha's father asked.

"We were rehearsing Act Two, Father."

"Oh, that's special," he replied. "Is that when Clara dreams? When the curtain opens on Act Two, the Angels float in circles, holding little green pine trees."

"I'm one of those Angels," said Willow. "I get to wear a white wig on my head, with a golden halo, and a long, full white dress. It's the Land of Sweets. There's a huge backdrop with candies painted on it. We give the Sugar Plum Fairy the good news of the Nutcracker Prince and Clara."

"I really like the Sugar Plum Fairy," said Julie.

"She's the ballerina from Italy," said her father. "The czar likes watching her dance."

"Did you hear that new sparkly instrument

yet?" asked Zack. "It's a celesta."

"No I haven't," said her father, "but all of St. Petersburg has been talking about Maestro Tchaikovsky's secret instrument."

"I watch the action from the side of the stage," I said. "After the Angels leave, the Sugar Plum Fairy waves her wand and dancers dressed as special treats come out. First, there's Hot Chocolate from Spain…"

"…then, there's Coffee from Arabia," burst out Zack, "and Tea from China."

"Luis comes out as a candy cane with bells on," I added.

"I had to jump through a candy cane hoop without tripping," said Luis. "It's not easy! I had to spring really high and spin the striped hoop."

The horse stopped, stomping its hooves in place. "I can't wait to see it," said her father. Musical notes from an accordion sang in the air. The burnt wood scent of bonfires and sweet Russian pastries swept around us. Tasha's father opened his hands. "Welcome to the Russian Fair! I think we'll find magic here."

And there was magic. It was like a carnival.

Colors of blue, red, green, and gold curled in the wind as the flags and signs waved on the little tents. Groups of people, both tall and short, were bundled in fur and wool. They hugged and laughed, holding mugs and steaming glasses of hot tea. Sellers called out, carrying wooden trays of lemon drops, candy sticks, and gingerbread cookies.

"Those are peddlers," explained Tasha. "They walk around selling yummy foods and toys."

A dog with golden fur ran over, barking at Julie. She bent down and stroked the back of its head. It licked her hands. "Tasha, come see," Julie said. "What a sweet puppy! I miss petting my dog back home."

"What's your dog's name?" asked Tasha.

"Ginger," I blurted out. Julie glared up at me. I gasped and closed my mouth. I had played with Julie's dog so many times.

Julie turned her back on me. "Ginger," said Julie to Tasha, just to make a point that what I said did not count. "She has golden fur, too."

"Check out the bear on the other side!" Zack pointed out. "I'm going there right now." His bubbly voice melted the tension.

Across the snow, a crowd had gathered around a brown bear on a leash.

"Wait a minute," said her father. "No running off. We must stick together."

"I want to see the puppets in the Petrouchka show," I said. I had heard about Petrouchka, a sad puppet who loved a beautiful girl puppet. But she loved someone else and broke Petrouchka's heart.

"We can do both," her father said. "But first of all, who's hungry?"

My tummy growled.

"Let me treat you to the best sweets in the world."

We followed him to a little stand. An old woman in black, peeked out from under a rosy scarf. She handed us a brown paper bag of donut-like pastries.

Tasha's eyes lit up. "I love to eat these."

As we bit into the crusts, white crystals of sugar spilled onto our fingers.

"Okay, Zack," said her father. "Your turn. Lead us to the bear."

We walked right next to the bear, in the front of the crowd. It was like a gigantic furry dog.

"Egor, Egor!" yelled the trainer, calling out the bear's name and giving a stiff tug on its leash. It rose up like an awakening giant, on its hind legs, paws high.

Then the man dangled a piece of meat on a string. The bear waddled on its back legs, batting the meat with its front paws. It was almost dancing. Our mouths dropped open.

"Now I've seen everything," Zack said.

"Haven't you seen a bear dance before?" Tasha asked.

"Once, at a circus," said Zack, "but not this close."

I chimed in, "That's how I felt in my mouse costume. Round and fur covered." We laughed.

The soft sounds of a violin came from the next little hill. Flashes of red satin spun, and black hair flowed as gypsies danced around a campfire. Armfuls of gold bracelets flashed on the women while some of the children kept time with their tambourines. The man playing the violin rocked back and forth.

Down the surrounding slopes, children whizzed on their wooden sleds, screaming and laughing. Boom-boom. Tap-a-tap-tap! Drumming filled the air.

"The puppet show starts soon," her father announced.

We followed the pulsing sound. Two drummers marched in front of a larger wooden building shouting, "Come one, come all! See Petrouchka fall in love." Little bright blue flags waved from the top towers. Red and purple curtains covered the stage. The Old Magician popped out, with his pointy wizard's hat and robes flowing into the square. He played a sad tune on his flute. The curtains, painted with gold flecks, slowly opened.

Life-size marionettes with strings and bright costumes bounced on the huge stage. Petrouchka wore baggy white pants that spilled over his red boots. His white clown hat hid his droopy face. One of his mitts covered his heart. He was bent over in sadness.

He loved the fancy ballerina puppet with the black curly hair and pretty long eyelashes.

She twirled with the Dark Moor in his golden turban. She ignored Petrouchka, breaking his heart. We clapped and laughed, even though Petrouchka never got the Ballerina.

As we left the puppet show, we saw a row of fir trees for sale. Some were lit with little candles that glowed against the whiteness of the snow.

Wham! Something hit my back. "Ouch." I spun around. Luis was laughing.

"You rat!" I yelled. I gathered up snow, just as Zack threw another one at my leg.

Willow flung a snowball at Luis. Snow flew back and forth as we ducked and dodged the balls.

Then I saw it. Julie and Tasha stood at a nearby jewelry stand. A young girl in a flowered shawl was selling trinkets. Tasha bought a necklace and fastened it around Julie's neck. The little golden brown crystals glowed.

I felt a pang in my stomach. Julie gave Tasha a hug of thanks. Just like BFFs.

Willow's snowball hit my fur hat. I barely felt it. She ran over. "What's going on? You've been frozen for the past minute."

I dropped the snowball and shook my head. "Nothing," I said.

Julie ran over to show off her gift. "Look at the necklace Tasha bought for me. She said these little stones are called amber."

Bam! A snowball hit my shoulder. Zack and Luis laughed.

"Watch out," said Julie as she leaned to one side.

Willow turned. "We're done, guys. The game's over."

"Says who?" shouted Zack.

I could not stand to be near Julie for one more second. I had to get away.

Luis held out his arms, daring us to hit him. "You can't get me, chickens!"

"I'll show him," I said. I ran with my snowball. Zack and Luis ran away from me. I flung my snowball hard at Zack.

He ducked and then it happened.

The snowball hit a tall man standing behind them, right in his back.

The young man turned. It was Yury! That horrid soldier I crashed into when I was a mouse, tripping him in the ballet. He squinted his eyes and frowned.

"You again! I don't believe it." He walked towards me. My stomach did a flip.

Then it got worse. The two girls standing next to him spun around. Denise and Nancy! Then the lady standing with them turned and looked at me. It was Miss Sophia!

17
The Amber Necklace

I stopped in my tracks. The boys froze, too. "Uh oh," said Zack.

Miss Sophia walked toward us, followed by Yury and the Mean Girls. Her chin nodded five times.

My stomach rolled. Willow was out of breath by the time she reached me. "Marti, what just happened?"

I was speechless. My stomach did a deep sea dive.

"What's going on?" Miss Sophia asked.

My cheeks felt hot. I shrugged.

Yury pointed. "It's her again."

"Marti, why are you throwing snowballs?" asked Miss Sophia. Then, she looked at Zack and

Luis. "This isn't Ballet Buster behavior. You're guests here."

"It's my fault," Zack said.

"No," said Luis. "I threw the first snowball."

"But I joined in," I admitted.

Miss Sophia said, "I'm disappointed in all of you. Marti, you owe Yury an apology."

I stepped forward through the snow. He didn't smile. "I'm so sorry, Yury, it was an accident. I won't do it again."

"Okay," he said with a frown. Then he turned and walked over to his friends.

Miss Sophia spoke to Tasha's father, their backs to us.

"Wow," said Denise. "You act just like babies."

"We were just having a little fun," Luis said.

"Look at my new necklace," Julie said to Denise and Nancy.

"No big deal. It's just amber," said Denise. "You can get it anywhere. I have an amber bracelet at home."

Nancy's voice dripped syrup. "Seems like you and Tasha are the new BFFs," she said to Julie. That stung.

"I didn't think we could take gifts from the Russians," said Denise, a know it all, like a peacock puffing out its silvery feathers. "We can't take anything back through the Ballet Buster Super Time Tunnel. You'll have to leave it here. Might as well just give it back to Tasha now."

Julie's voice was low. "This necklace is special to me," she said.

"If you say so," said Nancy. "Enjoy it. It won't last. Let's get out of here, Denise."

A moment later, Tasha and her father joined them. "Well Julie, great news," he said. "Miss Sophia said you could spend the night with Tasha!"

The girls looked at each other and jumped up and down, giggling.

The toes of my new boots felt cold and damp.

"The sleigh will drop us off at our apartment and then take the rest of you back to your rooms," Tasha's father said.

اللّٰه

The little bells tingled as the sleigh rocked. We stopped on a street with smaller buildings, all in a row. Tasha and her father climbed out in front of their arched doorway. Julie followed, laughing. She even forgot to say goodbye.

Zack and Luis moved over and sat on the bench across from Willow and me. The boys pulled the blankets up to their necks.

"We're sitting far away from you, Marti," Luis said.

"Yeah," said Zack, "we don't want you throwing any snowballs at us!"

"Thanks a lot, guys," I said. "Not funny."

After a while, the swaying of the sleigh put the boys to sleep.

In my mind, I replayed the movie over and over ... Tasha giving Julie the golden necklace and how they hugged, again and again.

"You're so quiet," said Willow. Her eyebrows lifted and her brown eyes open wider. "A penny for your thoughts."

I shrugged and looked down at my muff.

"Oh come on, tell me," said Willow. "What's wrong? Is it the necklace?"

I gulped. "Yes," I said. I took a breath. "It was hard seeing Tasha doing that. I know I broke Julie's trust when I threw her doll backstage, but I did say I was sorry."

My eyes watered.

"I know," Willow said.

"I can't reach Julie," I continued. "I've tried to make better choices, and she has cut me out of her life." I wiped away a tear. "We don't need to be BFFs. I just want to be her friend again."

Willow touched my arm. "Don't cry, Marti. Your tears will freeze."

"I wish I could give something to Julie, then she'd see I'm trying. But I don't have anything to give her. I can't buy her a necklace. I can't buy her anything."

"Even if we don't have money, maybe you can make her something."

The ice on the river glowed in the moonlight.

"You know what?" I said. "I'm an artist. I could draw her something."

"Yes, a picture would be good. Maybe do something from the festival," added Willow.

Then it popped into my brain. "I could draw a picture of Ginger. She left her dog's photo at home and really misses her."

That night, after Willow went to sleep, I sat at the little wooden table. I sketched by the candlelight. Ginger came to life with each pencil stroke. I erased and fixed the nose, working until her eyes smiled. I turned over the paper and wrote on the back, NEVER LOOK, EVER! It was not finished, and I did not want anyone peeking.

Before I crawled into bed, I saw the photo of my family.

"Abuelita, I'm trying to set things right. But it's so hard. I hope Julie loves my sketch of Ginger. You wouldn't believe all the snow. So much, we could throw snowballs. Night night."

My head hit the pillow. Then I remembered what Abuelita always said, "You need rain for rainbows." Good things can happen out of bad.

"I need a rainbow," I whispered.

18
The Rainbow

Knock, knock! I bolted upright in bed. The room blurred through my squinty eyes. Morning light peeped through the lace curtains.

"What's that?" asked Willow, lifting her head. Someone's at our door."

I tiptoed across the freezing wooden floor. "Who's there?" I asked.

"Miss Sophia. May I please come in?"

I gingerly opened the door.

"Good morning girls. Time to rise and shine. We have a big day today. It's our dress rehearsal. *The Nutcracker* opens in a couple of days." She glanced at the empty bed. "I stopped by to make sure you were both all right without Julie."

"I was fine, Miss Sophia," said Willow, "But Marti stayed up late. She was drawing."

Miss Sophia looked at the NEVER LOOK, EVER! sign on the table.

"Hmmmm, NEVER LOOK, EVER," Miss Sophia read out loud. "Marti, I guess it's yours?"

"Yes. It's something I drew for Julie. But it's not done yet. I want to show her I'm still her friend."

"Okay," said Miss Sophia. "Remember, Denise's big day is today. The people in the first *Nutcracker* didn't call her dance the 'Waltz of the Flowers.' Did you know that? It was called 'Waltz of the Sweetmeats.'"

"Sweetmeats.." Willow's eyebrows shot up. "What, does Denise wear a maple sausage on her head?"

We both laughed.

"No," said Miss Sophia, her eyes sparkling. "They called candy Sweetmeats, so you must not say 'Waltz of the Flowers' to Tasha or her friends. This is very important."

"Okay," they both said.

"Good," said Miss Sophia. "Now get going. See you at the theatre." She whirled out and shut the door.

Willow looked at me. "Brace yourself," she said. "We can't stand Denise on an 'okay' day. And, with her big dance, she'll be puffed out and proud as a peacock."

"I know. How will we ever stand her?"

Willow sighed. "It's going to be a long day. Don't forget to pack Ginger!"

"Let me fix Ginger's ears first. Then it'll be ready." I threw it in my bag. "Here goes nothing."

ele

The backstage was dark. Dancers rushed everywhere. I spied Zack standing next to Tasha. Willow and I had already changed into our ballet clothes. We headed over to Zack, dodging dancers left and right. As we got closer, Julie stood on the other side of Tasha.

"Hi guys!" We had to shout over the sounds of the instruments tuning up. Violin bows whipped through the air. The players in the orchestra sat in the pit below the front of the stage, lower than the audience, to not block the view.

Julie wouldn't even say "hi" to me. Every time she ignored me, a sliver of ice stabbed my heart.

Then I had a chilling thought. "What if Julie doesn't like my sketch of Ginger? What if she gives it back?"

"Watch out back here," said Zack. "Master Ivanov is on a rampage. He keeps on saying we aren't ready. On top of that, they are still sewing costumes."

Tasha added, "Master Tchaikovsky has to repeat the music again and again. Everyone is upset and worried. There are only a couple of days left for rehearsals, and this ballet has to shine. I think it's because the czar and his family will be there."

I pointed to seats in the theater. There was a fancy decorated place for people to sit and watch the ballet, high above the audience. "Does the czar sit in that gold box with those light blue shiny drapes?"

"Yes," said Tasha. "He comes on opening night. Often his wife and children come, too. He has a special entrance, near the side of the back-stage.

Suddenly, we were interrupted by shrill voices. The Mean Girls were at it again.

"Ouch, this button pokes my back. Fix it!"

Of course it was Denise, whining to Nancy about her costume. Denise put her hands on her waistband and pushed.

"Stop being so bossy," Nancy said.

Zack turned to us and whispered. "Wow, listen to Nancy. Who knew the Queen of Mean's minion could give it back?"

"Hurry up," snapped Denise. Her headpiece balanced on her bun.

"I'm going as fast as I can," said Nancy. "Quit snipping at me."

The other Sweetmeat dancers gathered next to Denise. The music swelled, and WHOOSH, they all moved onto the stage. Denise was actually doing a good job. I could not stand her bullying, but she was an excellent dancer. There were tricky turns and she hit them all. Denise swayed in a gigantic circle with the other Sweetmeats. Then she swished into the center and out again. Flowing skirts of purple and pink moved in and out.

The music got louder and grander. It played on and on. Finally, the dancers took their last pose and the notes ended.

Then it happened. As Denise left the stage, I heard a SNAP! I looked at Denise's ankle. The ribbon on her ballet slipper had popped open. She bent down to grab it. It caught under her other heel, and BAM, she tripped and fell down hard, her foot twisting under her.

"Owww!" she yelled, rocking back and forth in pain.

Miss Sophia ran over and stooped down. "Oh no Denise, where does it hurt?"

"It's my ankle." She started crying in pain. "Oh no, oh no."

"Poor dear," said Miss Sophia. "Your ankle is already swelling up." She quickly nodded her chin three times. "May I help you get up?"

Just as she bent down, Yury ran over. I could not believe my eyes.

"Mademoiselle, may I help?" he asked.

"Yes please," Denise said, weakly.

He firmly lifted Denise to her feet. What a strange sight. It was as if a Russian Wolfhound was leading a fancy little poodle to safety. Jealousy bubbled up in my tummy. It was hard to see Yury be so kind and gentle to my enemy.

Denise limped and sobbed on Yury's arm. I almost felt sorry for this Mean Girl.

As they passed, Nancy stood next to Tasha and whispered with a grin, "I bet Denise's hurt bad. If she can't dance, I'll get Denise's part. Good thing. I know all her steps!" She threw back her head with a short laugh.

Miss Sophia heard her and looked back. "Nancy, that laugh wasn't from you, was it? It didn't sound very nice."

Nancy straightened up. She blushed. "Oh no, I'm so sad for my good friend," she lied. Then she followed Miss Sophia to the dressing room.

"Whoa, did you hear Nancy laugh?" asked Zack. "What a mean friend!"

"Yes," said Willow in a low voice. "Who knew she's even mean to her BFF?"

"With a friend like that," I said, "a kid doesn't need an enemy."

"Well, when you're mean to everyone," said Zack, "you end up with that kind of friend."

"Yeah," I said. "Someone who tries to steal your part when you're injured."

Zack added, "Maybe Denise will be okay."

Willow looked at me with wide eyes. "Hey Marti, you should give your drawing to Julie now. She's not onstage for a while."

"You're right. I almost forgot."

I pulled the big brass handle of the wooden dressing room door. Miss Sophia was holding a bag of snow on Denise's ankle. In St. Petersburg, there are no freezers for ice. Denise was sitting on a bench, sniffling. I couldn't believe my eyes. Nancy sat next to her with sad eyes, holding Denise's hand, pretending to care.

"Excuse me," I said, grabbing the piece of paper from my bag and dashing out.

Julie was still backstage, standing next to Tasha. The stage light shone on the red satin bow in her light hair. She looked perfect, like a doll come to life. Julie and Tasha had their arms crossed, as they whispered to each other.

I took a deep breath. "I must try to give her

Ginger. If she doesn't like it, at least I tried."

I walked over and tapped Julie's arm. "Oh Zack, cut it out," Julie said with a smile. Then she turned and saw me. Her face dropped. "Oh, it's you."

I had nothing to lose.

"Julie, I have something for you," I blurted out. "I made it last night."

I thrust the drawing at her. Julie took it and peered closely at the pencil sketch.

The corners of her mouth curled up. "Oh Marti, it's Ginger! You made her just for me. Tasha, my dog looks just like this." She showed the paper to her friend. Then the unbelievable happened. Julie gave me a hug!

"I knew you forgot her photo," I said, "and I saw at the fair that you really missed Ginger."

"Let me see," said Zack, grabbing the drawing out of Julie's hands. "Wow, Marti, you're really good. It looks like Ginger could jump off the paper!"

"I just want us to be …" I began, but Miss Sophia came over.

"You must all get back to the dorm yourselves. I'll be with Denise. The Imperial Ballet doctor will take a look at her."

"What if...well what if she can't dance?" asked Zack. Leave it to Zack to say what was on everyone's minds.

"We'll cross that bridge when we come to it," Miss Sophia said. She nodded four times.

Zack squished his eyebrows together. "What does that mean?"

"It means we'll take one thing at a time. I need you all to be Ballet Busters and get to your rooms safely. Dinner will be waiting."

19
Tears for Denise

The next morning I walked into a small rehearsal room. Miss Sophia smiled, but kept on marking, or brushing through the steps of the waltz. In the dingy mirror on one wall, I saw Willow shaking out her arms to warm up. Nancy was in a split on the floor, putting clips in her hair. Denise sat in a corner chair, next to the violinist. Her head was down, while her ankle was wrapped in white cloths. A wooden crutch laid on the floor next to the chair.

Miss Sophia took a breath and smoothed out the silver streak in her hair. "Well girls, you're all here because Denise can't dance. We're sad about this, but the show must go on."

Miss Sophia's kind eyes looked at the injured dancer, whose eyes were red-rimmed, as if she had been crying. A small cotton handkerchief was bundled in her hand to wipe her tears.

I was not sad about Denise, but I kept quiet. Sometimes kids who are mean get what they deserve.

"Nancy, you'll replace Denise," said Miss Sophia. Nancy stood up with a grin. She acted like a pretty cat, purring sweetly after eating the mouse.

"Willow and Marti, I'm sure you're wondering why you're here," continued Miss Sophia. "You're both understudies. This means you'll learn the Sweetmeat part also. Then, if something happens, we'll still have a Ballet Buster onstage. I don't want Master Ivanov to put a Russian dancer in the dance at the last minute."

The violinist played the first notes. Miss Sophia moved across the floor. Her arms floated above her head as she counted out the beginning notes, "five, six, seven, eight."

Nancy, Willow, and I placed our hands to our

sides when Miss Sophia said "and." Our faces looked to the right. On "one, two, three, four," we moved through the space. Our feet traced the same path.

Miss Sophia's hands clapped three times. "Stop." she said to the violinist. "No Nancy, you must begin on the right foot at the count of one. Then brush the left foot through."

"No." Nancy shook her head. "You're wrong. The step begins on the left."

Willow and I looked at each other. We were shocked to hear Nancy talk back to Miss Sophia.

"No Nancy, I'm right. You're the one who's wrong," said Miss Sophia. "You're beginning on the left." Her head nodded three times. "Denise, what foot does the dance start on?"

"Um, the right foot," said Denise, in a little voice. She twisted her hankie in both hands.

Miss Sophia glared at Nancy. "Let's begin again on the right foot."

Nancy rolled her eyes and stepped to the side to begin again. She did the first couple steps.

CLAP, CLAP, CLAP. Miss Sophia stopped the dance again. "Nancy, your foot goes up to

151

your knee for that turn."

"I know," said Nancy.

"Well, please do it," said Miss Sophia. "We're running out of time. The costume mistress will measure you for your new costume after this."

Nancy shrugged.

Miss Sophia stopped and started a couple more times. Each time, the violinist put down his bow.

"Let's begin once more," said Miss Sophia. "No, no stop. Nancy, you must lift up your body when you turn. Reach your foot out to start the circle."

"I am!" Nancy said, with a huff, turning her back.

"Nancy, we need to have a little chat," said Miss Sophia. "Please come out here." She looked at us and the violinist. "Excuse us for a moment."

Nancy slowly dragged her feet across the floor, taking her time. Miss Sophia's arms were crossed.

Willow and I stretched on the floor. We overheard some of the words from the hallway. Miss Sophia did not sound pleased. "I don't like your attitude," she said. "You're being disrespectful." There were more whisperings we could not hear.

They both returned. Willow and I stood up. "I explained to Nancy we'll do the dance from the top," Miss Sophia said.

Strains of violin filled the room. We started on our right feet. About halfway through the dance, Nancy stopped and said to me, "No, turn the other way!" I kept moving.

"Enough, STOP!" said Miss Sophia. Nancy crossed her arms. Miss Sophia asked, "Denise, doesn't the circle step go clockwise, the way Marti is turning?"

Denise looked at her BFF, then turned her head toward me. She took a breath. "Miss Sophia, Marti was correct."

I was shocked Denise stood up for me.

"Girls, wait here a minute. The violinist and I need to talk about something." She whispered to the violinist, and they both walked out.

Nancy strutted up to Denise and looked down at her in the chair. "Well, thanks a lot. Why did you say I was wrong and Miss Priss over there was right?"

"Nancy, I had to tell the truth," said Denise. "After all we've been through, I don't want to give away my part to a Russian child."

"Well, if I lose this part," said Nancy, "it will be all your fault." Her eyes were on fire.

Miss Sophia and the violinist came back. "Girls," began Miss Sophia, "we're going to practice the dance until it is right. Tomorrow morning we'll meet backstage at Nancy's costume fitting."

With that, the violinist lifted his bow, and we started again and again. Willow and I were wiping sweat from the backs of our necks. Nancy danced the steps with just enough energy to move, but not too much effort.

A couple of hours later we took off our slippers in the dressing room. "I don't know why you both need to learn these steps," said Nancy. "This dance is mine. I know it. You're both wasting your time."

Before Willow or I could say anything, Nancy put on her coat. She flung her ballet bag over her shoulder and marched out of the room.

We stared at the door with our mouths open. We did not know what to say. Miss Sophia had asked us to learn the steps. Even if we were wasting our time, we did what Miss Sophia told us to do.

20
Trouble Finds Nancy

Each morning when we walked into the theater, we saw new things. Today, a small Russian woman waved her arms, yelling up to Miss Sophia. The white bun on the back of her neck bobbed up and down. Little silver sewing scissors, hanging on a red ribbon around her neck, jumped as she spoke.

Miss Sophia's mouth made a straight line. Looking down at the little yelling lady, she nodded her head the most times ever, clearly not pleased.

I felt a tap on my shoulder. "What Zack?" I asked.

"How did you know it was me?"

"Because," I said with a sigh, "nobody else sneaks around like that."

He shrugged. "Oh well."

"Hey, who's yelling at Miss Sophia?" asked Willow.

"That's the costume mistress," Zack said. "She's in charge of all the costumes. She's here to fit Nancy in her new costume, but guess who's late for her fitting?"

I looked at Zack with raised eyebrows. Before I could say Mean Girl number two's name, somebody brushed past, almost knocking me off my feet.

"Hey Nancy, look where you're going!" yelled Zack. Then he whispered, "Someone's in trouble. Take a look."

He was right. Nancy was out of breath and stood in front of Miss Sophia.

"Where have you been?" asked Miss Sophia. "You're late for your costume fitting!"

"I was fixing my hair," began Nancy. "I didn't think it was that important. It'll just take a couple stitches to make Denise's costume fit me."

The costume mistress crossed her arms. She

glared at Nancy.

"If you cared more about your new part, you'd know Madame is making you a new costume," said Miss Sophia. She gave one big nod.

Nancy looked down and gulped. "Well ... I... um ..." Her ears began to turn red.

Miss Sophia put her hands on her hips. The white streak in the front of her hair glowed silver.

"I've never seen Miss Sophia this mad," whispered Zack.

"You haven't been behaving like a Ballet Buster since Denise hurt her ankle," said Miss Sophia. "I've had enough of your rudeness." She walked over to speak with the costume mistress.

The three of us stood by the mice costumes hanging on the rack. The long black tails tickled our backs. We were dying to know what the adults were saying but were too far away to hear.

"Nancy," called out Miss Sophia. Please come here."

Nancy quickly walked over, her ears on fire.

"You've left me with no choice," said Miss Sophia with a nod. "I'm sorry, but I'm taking away your part."

We all gasped.

"No, please don't," begged Nancy. "I promise I'll be better. Please…oh no…please…"

"You were mean to Denise when she first hurt her ankle," said Miss Sophia.

Nancy wiped away a tear.

"Then you were awful yesterday at the special rehearsal," said Miss Sophia. "You made the others feel they were wrong, though you were the one who was not right. Now you're late for your new costume. I'm so disappointed in you."

Nancy sniffled.

"*The Nutcracker* ballet will not wait." Miss Sophia paused and looked into Nancy's eyes. "It's not always about you. You must never forget you're a Ballet Buster." Miss Sophia reached into her pocket and handed Nancy a white hankie.

"Nancy," said Miss Sophia. She sounded a little sorry for her. "You must make better choices. Now go and get ready for your Snowflake part."

"Okay, Miss Sophia," sniffled Nancy through her tears. "I'm so sorry." She slowly turned and walked toward the dressing room.

The costume mistress stepped over to Miss

Sophia and tapped her on the arm. "I know you've had some sadness here, but I need to sew a Sweetmeats costume right now."

"Yes, you're right," said Miss Sophia. "I need to decide on the new Sweetmeats dancer. Please give me a minute."

Madame threw up her hands and began fussing with the tails on the mice costumes. We edged out of the way.

"Hmmmm…We have no time to lose." Miss Sophia looked over at us.

"Marti and Willow, don't leave here."

"What about me?" squeaked out Zack.

"Oh Zack, you always have to be in the middle of everything," Miss Sophia said, smiling. "Stand to the side and out of the way."

A Ballet Buster was needed to jump into the Sweetmeats part.

My heart raced in my chest. What if I get the part after all? It would be a dream come true. It would be my rainbow.

"Willow and Marti, would you please come here?" Miss Sophia asked. "You both heard what happened."

We shrugged. Zack stayed to the side and pretended to look around. But we knew he was listening.

Miss Sophia continued. "We can't lose this chance to be in the first Sweetmeats dance. You have both worked very hard."

She looked right at me. "Marti, you made an awful choice tossing that baby doll backstage. But you've tried to make up for it."

Then she turned to Willow. "You're new to Ballet Busters, and you missed our first trip through the Super Time Tunnel. But, you've stepped up and done your best. There is one worry about you."

Willow's eyes got big. "What?"

"There are double *pirouettes* in this dance, which means you turn two times on one leg. You've just learned them. I'm not sure you can handle these in front of an audience."

"I'd like to try," said Willow.

With one nod, Miss Sophia made up her mind. "So this chance goes to …"

21

A New Sweetmeat

I gulped. Please let it be me, I whispered to myself. I wanted the Sweetmeat part to go to me.

"So this chance goes to …," said Miss Sophia with a smile, "… you, Willow."

"Oh wow!" Willow threw up her hands. "Lucky me!"

Miss Sophia gave her a pat on the shoulder.

"Good for you, Willow!" yelled Zack, from behind the hanging mice costumes. I knew he was peeking. Zack walked over. "You'll nail those turns. I know it."

My heart sank. I felt a tear sting my eye. But I remembered my Abuelita. She would want me to act grown up. I had to get myself together. I was a Ballet Buster. I took a breath.

"Nice job," I said, trying to sound upbeat. My voice felt wavy. "You'll be great."

"There's no time to lose, Willow," said Miss Sophia. "It's a relief you're Denise's size, so the costume mistress won't have to sew you a new costume." Miss Sophia grabbed Willow's hand and they left.

I brushed the fingers below my eyes to make sure there were no tears. I could still feel my heart beating. Back to being only a mouse, just my crummy luck. More rain for me. No rainbows.

"Hey, wait up." I turned and Zack was rushing to me. "I'm glad for Willow, but it's too bad for you. You almost had it…"

Then I heard Miss Sophia's voice. "Marti!" She was running back. "I forgot to mention, I still want you to understudy the role. You never know what will happen. Be at the afternoon rehearsal after lunch."

22
Willow's Spins

Willow and I stood next to each other in the darkness. The stage lights beamed on the stage. Everyone was jumpy and tense. Willow's shoulders shook with fear under her white ballet tunic. Master Ivanov, with his little glasses and graying hair, stood in the middle of the wooden floor. He clapped his hands and pointed at some of the dancers.

"I'm scared," Willow whispered in my ear.

"Don't worry," I said. "It'll be all right."

I said that, but inside I was wondering about Willow. She seemed so nervous. There were so many fast turns in the Sweetmeats waltz. This was the last Sweetmeats practice before the real performance. The next evening the czar and his family would watch the world's first performance of *The Nutcracker*, with the Ballet Busters.

The conductor faced the musicians in the orchestra pit. He tapped his little baton on the music stand in front. The musicians played the notes again and again.

"Willow, let's practice your turns right now," I said. "It might help you."

"Are you sure? It's really dark here offstage," she said. "I'm so nervous I can't think."

"This might help you calm down," I replied. "Look at me and do a turn."

Willow placed her feet apart and bent her knees in *demi plié*. She stared at my eyes, spun, and fell off the turn.

"See, I can't do even one turn," said Willow. "I just can't do it."

"Miss Sophia says, 'if you say you can't do it, then you never will,'" I replied. "You need to spot. Pick something to look at and turn your head fast. Super fast. Look at my face and just spot."

Willow stared at me and snapped her head around.

"Good," I said. "That was better. Now try two in a row."

Willow spotted two times. The first was good, but during the second turn her eyes drifted and she fell off her straight turning leg.

"See, I'm no good at this.

"Don't say that. Spot again. Try to spring off on your back leg when you turn. Go for two again."

Willow stared at me, one arm in front. She bent her knees and hopped on the second turn.

"See that was better," I said. "Try it again."

She did two turns and landed perfectly.

"Here, high five." We hit hands in the air.

"Girls, nice work!" We turned around and there was Miss Sophia. "Marti, you're a true Ballet Buster. I like how you helped Willow with her *pirouettes*."

"I think I can do it," said Willow.

"Do your best," Miss Sophia said. "The dance begins soon."

The Ballet Busters watched the waltz off to the side. Tasha stood next to Julie. Then, Zack ran over. "Go for it, Willow. We're all pulling for you."

"Break a leg," I whispered in Willow's ear. It was the performer's saying for 'good luck.'" Willow got in line with the others to enter the stage, smoothing down the loose hairs in her bun. She didn't smile. She looked as if she were being forced to leap through a hoop of fire.

The music began. Willow lifted her arms a little to the side and entered the stage. She flowed with the music, tracing all the steps we had practiced before. She hit every count perfectly.

Then came the turns in the circle. "Come on, Willow, do it," Miss Sophia whispered to herself.

I saw Willow take a breath before the first turn. She did two turns, but came out of it a little late, scrambling to catch up with the other dancers.

"Well at least she did two turns," said Miss Sophia.

For the next set, Willow began the first turn smoothly, but her ankle wobbled and she almost fell. Her shoulders lifted stiffly and she barely did the second turn. She was really nervous.

Willow was fine with the connecting steps.

There were two more sets of big turns. I watched her fix her eyes on a spot, but she still only did one turn.

"Pull it together," Miss Sophia said to herself.

Willow's eyes began to tear.

Then it happened. As she went into the last turn, Willow shook. She lifted up into it, but she fell off her foot, even before the turn. She pushed through the rest of the steps, but did not do the last turn.

Miss Sophia nodded her head four times and looked disappointed.

Zack walked over and stood next to me. We both glanced at Miss Sophia.

"This won't be good," she said.

I turned to Zack. "I tried to help Willow with her turns," I said.

"I know," he said, "but it's hard to be calm with so many people watching you. Poor Willow."

23

Maybe My Rainbow

Willow came offstage to Miss Sophia, covered her face, and burst into tears.

"I wasn't a Ballet Buster," sobbed Willow. "It was so hard."

"I know, I know," said Miss Sophia in a soft voice. She put her arm around her. "You are still a Ballet Buster because you did your best."

A tall young man with round glasses walked over to Miss Sophia. His mouth was in a straight line. "I'm helping Master Ivanov," he said. "He needs to see you onstage right away."

"Oh, I'm so sorry," said Willow.

"Please tell him I'll be right there," said Miss Sophia. She looked at Willow. "It'll be all right. Here." She handed her a handkerchief. "Dry your tears." Miss Sophia walked over to Master Ivanov.

Zack tiptoed over to listen to the adults, while I gave Willow a hug. Mr. Ivanov's hands were flying, and Miss Sophia kept nodding her head.

Zack scooted back to us, while Tasha approached.

"Zack," asked Tasha, "what were they saying?"

"I heard it all," he said. "Master Ivanov is mad, but Miss Sophia asked for one more chance. He said no, that we are out of time. Then Marti, guess what? Miss Sophia mentioned your name. That you should do it. You know it, and you're good at turns."

"Maybe this will be my big chance," I said.

Zack looked down.

"What Zack?" I asked. "What did he say next?"

"Mr. Ivanov said it's too late," Zack mumbled. "He was very disappointed you threw the baby doll."

"What?" asked Tasha. "That's not fair. Marti you can do it."

Tasha straightened up her body, so she

174

seemed to grow two inches. "I'm going out there to have a talk with Master Ivanov."

"Oh my goodness," was all I could say.

Tasha walked over to Master Ivanov and Miss Sophia.

"Master, may I please say a couple words?" asked Tasha. The ballet master stopped and looked down at her. His eyes were wide, as if he had seen a unicorn.

Tasha did not wait for him to say yes. "I know it's not my place, but Marti is an excellent dancer. She can easily do double turns. I know she did a foolish thing, but she feels awful about it. She has tried to make up for it."

Tasha gulped and added, "Master Ivanov, please give her a chance."

He looked over to Miss Sophia, who also had huge eyes. She nodded once.

Miss Sophia added, "Yes, Marti could do it. In fact, she's right over there. Could she show you her turns?"

Master Ivanov crossed his arms and squinted his eyes. "Miss Sophia, your dancers, the Ballet Bust…what?"

"Busters," added Miss Sophia.

"Yes, the Ballet Busters. They have been good, but I can't let your dancer be a Sweetmeat just to be nice."

"I understand," said Miss Sophia. "But if you saw Marti dance, you'd know she is right for the part."

"Please," Tasha pleaded.

"Little Tasha," said Mr. Ivanov. "I love your mother and father. They are some of our best dancers. And I've known you since you were a baby. Shaking his head, he said, "This is all too much."

"May I bring Marti over so you can see her?" asked Tasha.

"Oh all right," He winked at her. "For you, my little one, I will look."

Tasha ran over and grabbed my hand. "Marti, do your best. This is your only chance."

Zack burst out, "Break a leg, Ballet Buster!"

I was surprised that Tasha stood up for me.

I dashed into the bright lights of the stage, looked up and whispered, "Abuelita, please make me strong."

"This is Marti," Tasha said, presenting me to

Master Ivanov. I did a small bow.

His piercing dark eyes squinted through his tiny wire glasses. "Yes, let's see what you can do."

"Marti," said Miss Sophia. "Do the circle steps. He wants you to do the turns. I'll say the counts for you."

"Oh my," I thought. "That's the part with the double turns. Here goes nothing."

"Five, six, seven, eight," Miss Sophia said.

I pointed my right foot and lifted my arms softly to the side. I heard the music in my head. First turn. Whoosh.

Second turn. I snapped my head twice and kept dancing.

Third one. I solidly hit it.

Last one. Come on, you're almost golden.

I pointed my foot, picked my spot, turned twice, and easily sailed through it. After I finished the dance steps, I held my last pose.

Mr. Ivanov began clapping. "Well done, Little Marti."

I ran over to Miss Sophia, whose eyes smiled.

"We just have one problem," said Master Ivanov.

"What is it?" asked Miss Sophia. "She's also a mouse, but that is in the First Act. She'll have lots of time to change into her Sweetmeats costume."

"Marti is much smaller than the other girl," said Mr. Ivanov. "She'll need a new costume. We'll need it by tomorrow night."

"Oh," said Miss Sophia. Her shoulders sank. "This is a huge problem."

I knew it was too good to be true. I had my big chance, and now it was over.

Mr. Ivanov brushed a finger over his mustache and looked up. "I'll do what I can. I'll talk to the costume mistress. If she can sew a new costume by tomorrow night, Marti can do the dance. If not, I'll have to put in one of our dancers."

"Thank you, thank you," said Tasha, jumping up and down.

"I can't promise," said Mr. Ivanov. Then he turned and walked to the costume shop.

"Marti," said Miss Sophia, "I'll tell you about your costume as soon as I find out. Until then, try not to get too excited."

I let out a breath. Oh my. First I'm just a mouse, then I'm also a Sweetmeat, then seconds later, I'm just a mouse again. My Abuelita would not believe it.

"Oh and Marti," yelled Miss Sophia, "please look for Willow. I don't see her anywhere. I'm worried about her."

"Okay, I'll do that."

I felt a poke on my back.

Zack.

"Oh Marti, I would hate to be you," he said. "First you're nothing, then you're everything, and then maybe you're nothing again."

I heard a voice behind him. "Zack, you're mean! She's a Ballet Buster no matter what!" I turned my head and couldn't believe my eyes. It was Julie. "Marti, you did a great job in those turns. I couldn't have done it with all those people watching."

"Thanks, Julie."

I showed a small smile, but I was grinning big inside. I might have lost the best part ever, but I was getting my friend back.

"It takes rain to make rainbows," I said. "May-

179

be this will be my rainbow."

"Let's get back to the dorm," Zack said, "I'm starving."

"Wait a minute, don't go yet," Tasha called. "Willow's in the dressing room getting changed and she looks pretty down."

"Yeah," I said. "She must feel awful. She tried her best."

"I'll get her," said Tasha. "Julie, come with me. You all wait here. I'll tell you some good news in a minute."

Willow's brown eyes were red-rimmed. She bit her lip. I wanted to hug her, but since I took her Sweetmeat part, I felt like that was not the right thing to do.

"Cheer up, Willow," said Zack.

"Yes, cheer up!" said Tasha. I have great news."

24
Tasha's

Since we all need to be cheered up," Tasha said, "here's great news from my father. He has invited all of you to our apartment for dinner. We live only a couple blocks away, and my mother is a wonderful cook."

Zach scratched his head. "Isn't she a ballet dancer, too?"

"Yes, but now she teaches at the school. Let's share a yummy Russian meal tonight."

"I'll grab Luis," said Zack. "He just went to get his coat."

Outside, Tasha stood next to Willow, while Julie, Zack, and Luis strolled behind with me.

"Hey," said Tasha. "Let's walk to the Neva River and see if there are any ice skaters. It's close by."

As we walked, we could hear shouts, laughter, and the crunch of blades on the ice. As we leaned over the black lacy railing, lots of ice skaters, especially children, whizzed across the frozen surface. A little girl went plop on the ice and began to cry. Her father helped her up and quickly wiped a tear with his handkerchief. Two young boys chased each other across the crowded river, almost knocking over an older couple on skates.

Then we saw little boy and girl on a sleigh, pulled by two big dogs. The little girl held out a long stick. The stick had a piece of meat attached to it, which dangled in front of the dogs. The dogs ran faster and faster as they tried to grab the piece of meat. But they never did reach the food!

"Well, now I've seen everything," laughed Luis.

Willow giggled. "I bet those dogs are still hungry."

I was glad to hear Willow sounding more

cheerful. The evening might turn out all right, after all.

Julie pointed to me. "Marti, you should draw a picture of those two furry dogs."

Tasha spun around. "Here, follow me." We turned away from the skaters. "My father will let Miss Sophia know where you are. Then he'll walk you back home."

After passing a couple streets, Tasha stopped and knocked on the door in a tall brick building. We all crowded up the narrow stairs to the second floor. In the hallway, we sniffed the smell of warm fresh bread and the scent of sweet beets.

اللہ

The door to Tasha's home opened. "Welcome all," greeted her mother. Her light brown hair was pulled into a bun. A woolen shawl with large roses was wrapped around her shoulders.

After Tasha introduced us to her mother, I said, "I really love your pin." Her large oval brooch was gold with small rubies and pearls.

"Oh this," said her mother, as she fingered it.

"This was my mother's. Her father owned a jewelry store here in St. Petersburg."

We piled our coats and mittens on a carved wooden chair in the corner. Her apartment was small yet cozy, with a table in the center and a tiny kitchen to one side. Golden flames in the fireplace warmed the main room. Tiny bells chimed five times from a delicate clock on the mantle.

"Come and see my bedroom," said Tasha. Wooden walls enclosed a small room with a little bed, a dresser, and a bookshelf overflowing with books. Above that, she had a pair of worn *pointe* shoes hanging by its pink ribbons.

"Those were my mother's ballet slippers," pointed out Tasha.

"I love the pink satin covering the shoes," I said. "The tips are so little and pointy."

Tasha sat down on the floor in the middle of her room. She patted the soft woven rug of reds, purples, and yellows, on both sides of her. "Come sit on the rug," she said. "I need to tell you something."

Julie plopped next to Tasha, while we quickly

sat down.

"Miss Sophia talked to my father before we went to the Festival," Tasha began. "Later, my father told me what she said."

"What did Miss Sophia say?" asked Zack. I could tell he couldn't wait any longer.

"Okay, she told him your secret," whispered Tasha. "She said you're Ballet Busters from another time. From the future. That you traveled through the Super Time Tunnel. You'll dance in our first *Nutcracker*, and then go back home."

"She's right," said Willow.

"Did your father believe her?" asked Julie.

"Yes," said Tasha. "Even though you'll leave in a couple days, he said I could still be friends with you."

"Whew," said Zack. "We're glad he's letting you be with us."

"That's why my mother invited you for dinner," said Tasha. "She wanted to meet my special friends."

The front door opened in the main room, and her dad shouted, "I'm home!"

Tasha jumped up and ran out of her bedroom

to give him a hug. We all followed.

"Dinner smells great," said her father. He hung his coat on a clothes tree, a tall wooden pole with hooks at the top.

"Tasha," said her mother, "have your guests take a seat."

We sat around the sturdy table in candle light. Her mother brought over a large tray with bowls of hot purplish soup, made from beets, called borscht.

"Here, have some sour cream," said Tasha's father. "You put a spoonful on top of the soup."

Zack grabbed a piece of black bread from the basket, and Luis passed him the butter.

"Would you like a cup of tea?" asked her mother. She went over to the samovar, a large metal pot that heated the water, and filled the little glasses with tea.

"Mother," said Tasha, "you won't believe what happened today." She told her about the excitement with the Sweetmeats dance.

"Willow," said her father, "I am proud you did your best. Those turns are very hard, even for older dancers."

"You saved the day, Tasha!" said Zack. "It took a lot of guts to go to Master Ivanov."

"I still can't believe I did it," said Tasha. She stirred a little sugar into her tea. "I thought I had nothing to lose. Marti, I knew you could do the turns."

"Thank you!" I said. "I can't believe I'll have to wait to hear if I have a costume. Tomorrow I'll find out."

"That's the way shows are," said Tasha's mother. "Sometimes you have to just hope for the best. It takes a lot of work to make just one dress. The costume mistress is always stressed just before the ballet opens."

"That little old costume mistress," said Julie, "was so funny when she jumped up and down with her tiny scissors on the ribbon. She looked like she might poke out her eye!"

"Maybe you'll get lucky," said Tasha's father. "There's an opera before we dance *The Nutcracker*. That'll give the costume women more time to make your outfit."

"There have been so many problems with this *Nutcracker*," added her mother. "First Master Petipa got ill. Then, Master Ivanov took over. Now there are complaints that the party scene children are too wild onstage. This is the first Russian ballet with so many younger dancers in it."

The moon's glow poked through lace curtains on the windows.

"Tasha," said her father, "play a song on the violin for your guests."

"Oh, do I have to?" asked Tasha.

Luis' eyes got wide. "Wow! You never said you could play the violin."

"All the dancers here have to learn to play music," her mother said. "Come Little One, I'll play with you."

Mother and daughter stood next to each other in front of the music stand. Tasha's mother lifted her violin to her chin, while Tasha picked up her miniature instrument. While we munched on gingerbread dessert, musical notes floated around us. It was beautiful.

Finally, it was time to leave. As Tasha's mother kissed me goodbye on both cheeks, she whispered, "I hope your costume is done in time. I can't wait to see you as a Sweetmeat."

"Thanks," I smiled.

Later that night, I tossed from side to side in my bed. Nothing felt comfortable. I heard Julie and Willow breathe deeply in their sleep.

In the moonlight, I looked at my photograph on the nightstand. Abuelita's face beamed back at me. I looked at her kind eyes.

Oh, I want SO much to be a Sweetmeat tomorrow. Please, please. I need my Rainbow.

The next morning after our ballet class, the news was not good. "No news yet, Marti," Miss Sophia said. The door was closed to the costume shop, and no one could look in. I heard voices and sewing machines clicking.

"Oh my goodness," I groaned. "I wish I knew ... either way. This is taking forever. I hate not knowing."

"Hang in there," said Miss Sophia. "I know it's hard."

We walked back to the theater after dinner. It was the big opening night in December of 1892.

Luis warmed up backstage. "Still no news, Marti?"

"None," I said. "Miss Sophia is beginning to

think my costume won't be done in time."

He did a couple jumps, pointing his feet hard. "I feel sorry for you."

I felt a poke on my back. I knew who it was. "Ouch!" I said, "Stop it, Zack."

I turned and there he was with the rest of my Ballet Buster friends.

"Sorry," Zack said, "but we wanted to do something for you. You need to take your mind off of everything else."

Tasha spoke first. "I have a plan. A secret plan." We all gathered around.

25

A Secret Door

In the darkness of backstage, Tasha shared her plan.

"Well," she began. "I know a secret door that leads up there." She pointed up past the lights above the stage.

"You're kidding," I said. "Why do we need to go up there?

"Because," said Julie, "we have a long, long wait before *The Nutcracker* starts."

Willow added, "We're on after the opera. And you know, we'll get bored just sitting around."

"I heard about this opera," said Luis. "In the old days, people would sit hours in the theater to watch many shows."

"So I plan to sneak up there above the lights," continued Tasha, "and look down on everything. We'll see most of the opera."

My heart raced. "But won't we get in trouble?"

"I never have," said Tasha, "and I've done it before."

"Who cares if we get in trouble?" asked Zack. "We're leaving tomorrow. And besides, they'd never think to look up there for us. When the opera is done, we'll scoot back down."

"They won't even miss us!" said Tasha. "There's just one catch."

"What's that?" I asked.

"We need to walk past the dressing rooms of the *prima ballerina* and the *premier danseur,*" said Tasha. "If they notice us, they might not let us dance."

"Won't we stand out?" asked Julie.

"Well, we can't walk by the dressing rooms like noisy silly kids," said Tasha. "We'll need to slip by." She glared at Zack.

"Well, that leaves me out," he said. "I need to act like myself, like a noisy silly kid."

"Just zip your mouth closed, Zack," Luis said. "Otherwise, it'll be a long time down here with nothing to do."

"Just follow me," said Tasha. "Walk like you belong."

We slipped out of the stage area and into the long white hallway. Men carried huge fake plants and golden furniture. We ducked.

"Those are props for the opera," whispered Tasha.

She led us to a door with a big gold star on it. "That's the *prima ballerina's* dressing room," she said. "She plays the Sugar Plum Fairy." Suddenly, Tasha put up her hand for us to stop.

Tasha's eyes opened wide, as if she'd seen a greenish ghost in the hallway. She stepped to one side and hid behind a marble statue. We squished in behind her.

"The czar!" Zack whispered.

A tall regal gentleman with a short brown beard in a dark suit paused at the door. A long black cape was draped over his shoulders. The woman who followed him had her hair swept up, held in place with a sparkly crown of diamonds. A long white fur was wrapped around her green satin dress. Two of their six children stood behind them, a teenage boy and a young girl. Snowflakes melted in their hair, as a man in a uniform stepped in from the outside and closed the door behind them.

"This is the czar's private entrance into the theater," whispered Tasha. "Look."

The dressing room door with the golden star opened. "I will get Mademoiselle." The small woman in a plain black dress bowed her head and turned.

"That's her maid," said Tasha.

The *prima ballerina* came to the door. Her eyes, outlined with black pencil, beamed at the czar. She pulled a silky red shawl around her shoulders. Her gleaming dark hair was halfway pulled into a bun. The czar stepped toward her, lifted her hand, and kissed it. We all bit our tongues, to keep from saying yuk.

"We look forward to a wonderful performance tonight," said the czar. "Here is my wife and two of my children." He put out his hand to them.

We didn't move a muscle. We barely breathed. Finally, the family walked out of the dressing room, and the door closed.

"Act natural," said Tasha. She turned and smiled at us, as if we were all walking to ballet class. The czar's family swished right past. I was so close I saw the emerald earrings flash on his wife's ears. His son looked down at me and glared.

We turned the corner. "Whew," said Tasha. "That was a close call. We could have gotten into a lot of trouble if the czar asked us why we were there. Keep moving."

We followed her down a long white hallway until she stopped in front of a larger wooden door with chipped paint and an old handle. She turned to us. "Here is my secret door. We're going to climb almost to the stars."

She opened it, and we walked up the steep wooden stairs, then down another hallway, which opened onto the edge of the stage. We were high above the wooden floor. The lights glowed. The singers below looked like mini people, dressed in velvet and lacy costumes.

"Follow me." She started up a black iron staircase. It had openings between the steps. "Don't look down!" she warned. We went up and up until we stopped at a long black iron bridge that went across the top of the stage. Now we were above the lights.

"This is called the cat walk," said Tasha. "That's because you have to be steady on your feet, like a cat. Don't fall between the iron rungs."

And she was right. I gazed out over the stage below. We were up so high we could see only the tops of the opera singers' heads. The footlights were a row of colored lights far below, shining across the wooden stage floor.

"Come out here and sit." We stepped carefully on the rungs and sat down.

"The ropes over there pull the curtains," said Luis. "You can see the slabs of bricks that are the weights. Those move up and down, so the men can open the heavy curtains."

The magic backstage made the story come alive. As they lowered scenery behind the performers, I turned and saw the top of the gigantic Christmas tree from *The Nutcracker*. It was in back, tied to a huge metal rod just below us. Later during the ballet, the tree would rise up, as it grew before Clara's eyes.

I felt like a bird in a tree, peering down. The opera had not started yet. The audience began to clap. We looked out at the audience. The fancy seats up in the first balcony were framed by pale blue curtains with thick golden tassels.

"Those are the box seats of the czar," said Tasha. "We'll watch his family sit down."

"Yes," said Julie. "It's as if our president or a queen came to watch a show."

The czar and his wife, with their children, stood at the edge of the railing and waved at the crowd. The people clapped loudly. Afterwards, the family sat down. Suddenly, blackness surrounded us. I saw the musicians in the orchestra pit, in front of the stage. The conductor came out and bowed. Again the audience clapped. He lifted his baton. The musicians picked up their violins and flutes. When the conductor lowered his baton, they began to play. The sound circled up and swirled around us.

"Those bricks slam down when the curtains

or backdrops are moved by the backstage men," Tasha warned. "It's going to be loud. Just hold on tight."

Bam! Boom!

I gasped! The men pulled down on the ropes to open the curtain. I jumped, as if a firecracker exploded next to me.

Zach smiled and sank lower. "It's noisy up here," he said, "but we have the best seats in the house."

The lights brightened below. The singers came onstage, and the opera began. We watched the tops of their hair and hats. Their voices floated up.

"In operas, they don't speak, they just sing," said Tasha. "The czar loves opera."

The huge lights below warmed our feet. The show came to life, below us.

I glanced in the wings, offstage. Then I saw them, the Mean Girls! They were pointing to the action on the stage when they looked up. Their mouths opened, and their beady eyes glared upward.

Oh no! Caught!

26
Close Call

Denise pointed at us and said something. She leaned on one crutch, while Nancy stood next to her. I couldn't believe they saw us.

I whispered to Tasha over the music. "Look! We're in trouble!"

Tasha groaned. "Oh no. We better get moving so no one else sees us. When the music gets loud, stand up slowly and move along the cat walk."

The opera singers bellowed over the horns and the taps of the drums. We stood up and carefully walked on the rungs. There was nothing but air between them. If we fell, we were gone. I glanced down at Denise.

Whoops! My foot slipped off the metal rung. I grabbed the metal rail with my hand as my leg fell below the cat walk. Bam! I hit the metal rung. My leg dangled below the cat walk.

I froze. Butterflies flew in my tummy.

"Hang on!" Willow breathed behind me. Her arms were on my waist. "Now Marti, slowly sit on both rungs. There. Bring up your leg."

I pulled my leg up and put my foot flat on the metal. My body shook. Zack took my hand. My stomach did circles. The singers' voices surrounded us.

"We have you," said Zack. "Steady. Slowly stand up."

I bent my knees and balanced on my feet.

"Good, you're up," said Tasha. "Now slowly step forward."

My ankles wobbled. One step at a time, I told myself. Don't look down! The stage was far below. It seemed like a wiggly rope suspension bridge high above a river.

"Eight more steps," said Tasha. I moved forward with the Ballet Busters and finally stepped off the cat walk. There was no time to catch my breath. We followed Tasha down the stairs and looped through the hallways. Tasha pulled the handle on the secret door and poked her head out to look both ways.

"The coast is clear," she said. We followed her backstage.

Just our luck, Denise was standing at the stage door, puffed up. "Miss Sophia has been looking for you everywhere," she said in her whiny voice. "Wait until she hears you were up on the cat walk and almost fell through. What a fool!" she laughed.

I glared at her.

"Oh, guess what?" asked Nancy.

"What?" I really couldn't stand them.

"Your costume isn't done and probably won't be," she said. "So there!" And they both turned. Nancy helped Denise limp away on one crutch.

I felt like a basketball had slammed into my stomach.

My shoulders dropped. Then I saw Miss Sophia. "There you are. We were looking all over for you. Where have you been?"

"It's a long story," said Zack.

"We don't have time to hear it now," Miss Sophia said.

"The costume mistress thinks your dress won't be done," explained Miss Sophia. "I'm so sorry, Marti. They put one of their dancers in a larger costume. She'll be the Sweetmeat tonight."

My teacher put her hand on my shoulder. "But after you do the mouse, I want you to put the headpiece on for Sweetmeats ... just in case."

Miss Sophia leaned over and looked in my eyes. "There's still a small chance the costume will be done."

I sighed, straightened up and turned to my friends. "There's nothing I can do right now. Let's get changed, so we're ready."

Mouse costume, here I come.

The girls' changing room buzzed like the inside of a bee's nest. Children hopped around in white petticoats, puffy skirts, and pink tights. The women in black dresses, who helped with the costumes carried shimmery red skirts and rainbow-colored tutus. On the racks hung blue party dresses with lace, snow costumes with glittery tops, and red-striped candy cane outfits.

Before I knew it, the brown furry mouse outfit was yanked over my head. I waved the tail behind me.

"Careful. You're going to kill someone with that!"

I looked over. It was Willow, dressed in her sparkly white angel costume. A golden halo popped up above her hair.

I hoped she was not mad at me for almost taking her part.

"Sorry about the Sweetmeats," I said.

"It wasn't your fault. You aren't even sure if you'll be dancing it."

"Miss Sophia thinks not. But I still need to be ready to go onstage, even if it's at the last minute."

"Yes, we always need to be ready," said Willow. "We're Ballet Busters."

"Well, tomorrow at this time we'll be back at home," I added.

"I miss my mom," said Willow.

"FIVE MINUTES TO PLACES!" yelled the stage manager. He made sure the dancers were ready backstage.

Finally, the first performance of *The Nutcracker*. We had traveled through the Ballet Busters Super Time Tunnel for just this moment. I stood in the dark shadows with Zack and Willow watching the action onstage, my costume ballooning around me, a fat brown mouse from the neck down. Even though I was nervous about dancing, I was thrilled to hear the first sounds of the ballet. The violinists strummed short, quick notes.

Out of the blackness, lights burst above the stage. It was as if the sun had come through dark rain clouds, while the story was told with movements only.

Act I came to life as party guests walked onstage. The dancers, who practiced in ballet outfits with dull tops and faded tights, wore bright velvet dresses and black suits with top hats.

Julie and Tasha skipped out with the adult dancers, carrying large presents to give at the party. Later, Julie cradled her baby doll.

That doll got me in so much trouble! I had made such bad choices. I wanted Julie's part so much that a monster grew inside of me. Jealousy had gobbled up all the good feelings I had.

As I watched the party scene, Julie spun around and hugged Tasha. I felt a sharp pang. That jealousy monster wanted to grow again, but I wrestled it away. I was just a mouse and probably wouldn't be a Sweetmeat.

I remembered my Abuelita. Her voice in my head said, "Do the right thing." So I chose to think about something else. I turned to Willow.

"Don't Julie and Tasha look happy together?" I couldn't believe I'd said it. But after those words passed out of my mouth, I felt better.

Willow smiled. "They both sparkle."

"We'll miss Tasha," I said, "and her parents."

"Poor Julie," said Willow. "And poor us."

"Yeah, and we'll miss Russia," Zach added.

Zack was right. We would miss St. Petersburg.

The scenes quickly passed. Before I knew it, Clara was sleeping on the stage. The dream part of the ballet began. My dreams might come true tonight, I thought. If only I could be a Sweetmeat. Hurry and sew my costume!

Zack tapped me on the shoulder. "Time for the mice and soldiers to line up."

I yanked my mouse head on and stood in

line. Do not crash into any soldiers, especially Yury.

I ran out into the pretend living room and passed the Christmas tree, feet jiggling up and down. I passed between the soldiers. They shot the cheese out and my feet sprang in little jumps. Boom! I was shot down and pulled off the stage.

I panted on the side of the stage, hot from the stuffy mouse head. On the bright side, I had done my mouse dance perfectly, so one of my dreams had come true.

Miss Sophia mouthed the words, "Not done yet." I knew what she meant. My costume was not finished. I was going to be a mouse forever.

Once inside the dressing room, the music changed. *The Nutcracker* became a Nutcracker Prince. I hung my puffy brown costume in the dressing room. I pulled on a leotard and fixed my hair and make-up, just in case.

The snowflakes, with their white puffy head-pieces and fluffy skirts rushed in to change. This was the end of Act I. With the curtain closed, the crew swept up the fake snowflakes and hung the scenery for the next act.

Willow's moment came as the Angel Dance opened Act II. The Magic Castle, where the Sugar Plum Fairy lived, was splashed across the back of the stage. Brushes of bright pinks and turquoises made the candies stand out in the Land of Sweets.

Clara arrived and the Nutcracker Prince used pantomime to tell about his adventure fighting the mice. After the Spanish dance, the Arabian section, and the Chinese Tea, Luis spun and leaped as a Candy Cane. I got worried my costume would never be ready.

I tried to smile. "Great dancing, Luis. You really jumped high."

"Thanks, Marti. What about you? There are only two more dances until Sweetmeats."

I looked at him and shrugged. I could not tell him my big chance was gone. We watched as Marzipan and her Shepherd Girls attacked the wooden floor on the tips of their pointe shoes.

Miss Sophia came toward me with a frown. A Russian dancer in a Sweetmeats costume walked next to her.

I felt doomed.

27
Doomed?

"Marti," said Miss Sophia, "I have bad news. The women sewing can't find the hooks that close your costume in the back. They said we must plan for this dancer to go on in your place."

The older dancer started brushing her feet to warm up while I looked at the dark wooden floor, blinking back tears. I would not cry.

Luis stood next to me. He knew the "Waltz of the Sweetmeats" came after Mother Ginger. We watched the children spill out from under Mother Ginger's skirt. These little clowns kicked and did cartwheels in their fancy costumes of purples, oranges, and pinks. My heart sank.

I heard voices behind me and turned. The short costume mistress with her little white bun was talking to Miss Sophia. The scissors around her neck hopped up and down. She held a needle and a spool of purple thread. Miss Sophia nodded her head four times.

"Quick!" said Miss Sophia.

Before I could say anything, the fluffy net costume was pulled down over my shoulders. Another older Russian woman straightened the headpiece on my bun. The hooks at the back of the dress were yanked together with thread. I was sewn into the Sweetmeats costume.

"They'll have to cut the threads to get you out of your dress," said Miss Sophia. She pushed me into the dancers standing by the curtain. "You're a Sweetmeat."

Goodness gracious!

"You can do it, Marti!" said Luis. The audience clapped at the end of Mother Ginger.

My heart thumped in my chest.

I had no time to think. The first notes of the waltz floated up from the orchestra, one, two, three and one, two, three. I stepped and swayed, matching the girl in front of me. On 'and' I lifted my arms slightly to the side. Our puffy rainbow colored skirts beamed under the lights.

I hit an *arabesque*, with my leg in back and my arms up. Then step, step. *Arabesque* on the other foot. As I moved toward the curtain, Zack whispered, "Break a leg, Ballet Buster."

The section with four turns was next. I had to get these spins right. I knew the Ballet Busters were watching me.

The first one came. Step, step, I pointed my foot. I lifted my leg up, spotted the girl in front of me, turned, but it was a bit slow. I did a couple quick steps to catch up.

Turn number two had a nice snap to it, but the third one was shaky. I almost fell off my foot. My mouth was dry. I could barely breathe. I needed to get this last turn. If I fell, it would be the worst. I had to find my inner strength.

I stepped into the fourth turn. My body lifted straight up, and I quickly pulled in my arms. One spin, two spins, and I smoothly moved into the next step. I hit it with two turns! My eyes glanced at the side. Miss Sophia smiled and did three nods.

Ta da! I finished the dance with my arms out. Clapping filled the air. We did a quick bow and ran offstage.

Tasha hugged me first. "Marti, you did it!"

Miss Sophia came over. "Those turns were great, Marti!"

Zack lifted his hand toward me and gave a high five.

"Quiet backstage," whispered Miss Sophia. "Let's watch the ending of *The Nutcracker*."

Willow gave me a quick hug, and Luis did a thumbs up. Then we turned toward the hot lights onstage.

The magic of the Sugar Plum Fairy and her Cavalier unfolded as we watched. The ballerina, with a short puffy dress, stretched and turned with her male partner. He even did small lifts. In this *pas de deux*, or dance for two, the man danced and then together they both did fast turns and leaps, ending in a grand pose.

Miss Sophia said, "Run out now." We all sped out onstage to say goodbye to Clara and the Nutcracker Prince. The Sugar Plum Fairy said goodbye to Clara with a kiss on her cheek, while the Cavalier kissed her hand.

Clara and her Prince waved goodbye from their sleigh. The last of Maestro Tchaikovsky's notes spun in the air. The conductor in the pit put down his baton. Heavy curtains thumped together. It was time for the final bows.

We ran behind the curtain to bow with the entire cast. Over 200 dancers lined up onstage. I stood next to the other Sweetmeats. Julie was up in front with Tasha and the party children.

The applause began. The stagehands pulled heavy ropes and the curtain opened. We stepped together to the side and bowed. The Sugar Plum Fairy and the Cavalier stepped in front for a special bow. People clapped even louder.

We bowed again. My dream of dancing a special part had come true. I felt just like Clara in *The Nutcracker*. She had wanted her nutcracker to be the Nutcracker Prince, and it happened. Both of our dreams had come true.

I walked offstage. Then, I bumped into Nancy.

"Be careful!" she said, reaching down and picked up Denise's crutch.

"Marti," began Denise.

I waited for my rainbow to flatten.

"You did a really good job with the turns in the Sweetmeats," she said.

"Yeah," added Nancy, "you did."

My mouth dropped open. "Thanks," I said.

"No really," said Denise, "you nailed those turns. They were hard. You're a real Ballet Buster."

I felt as if I had received a perfect score on a tough spelling test.

"Wow," Zack said. "I never thought I'd hear the Mean Girls say nice words."

"They made my day," I said. "But Zack, I can't believe you were listening. You're everywhere."

"Yeah," said Zack. "I know everything." As he sped off, he shouted, "And don't forget, we pack tonight!"

Walking out of the theater with my Ballet Buster friends, I glowed inside.

All snuggled in our fur hats and leather mitts, our sturdy boots clomped on icy stones in the moonlight, heading to our rooms to pack. I caught a cold snowflake on my tongue and smiled.

28
Goodbyes

Bam, Bam, Bam! "Wake up. Come on!" It was Zack. Always Zack. "The Ballet Buster Super Time Tunnel will not wait!"

"Okay!" I rubbed the sleepers out of my eyes.

"We need to pack," he yelled through the wooden door. "The magical trunk is in Miss Sophia's room."

"Willow, Julie, time to rise and shine. It's our big day," I said.

A ray of sunlight brightened the rug on the floor. The girls turned over in their beds, still sleeping.

"We need to get our things together and bring down our keys," I said.

Julie sat up and groaned. "I'm so tired. I want to go home and see Ginger, but I don't want to leave …" Her words got lost in her throat. She wiped away a tear.

"You mean you don't want to leave Tasha," added Willow. "And her mom and dad."

Julie nodded her head 'yes.'

"It's going to be hard," I said. "But we need to get packing."

I sprang out of bed, and the girls followed. We changed into our clothes, grabbed our keys, tossed our bags over our shoulders, and headed downstairs. Miss Sophia's door was wide open. Dancers tossed tights, slippers, and pajamas into the towering brown magical trunk. It shook with a low buzz. I tossed in the photo of Abuelita, Mama, and little sis Francesca. Julie threw in the picture I had sketched of Ginger. That made me feel good, like I had kicked the soccer ball into the net and scored. Julie and I were friends again.

This time, the sign on the side of our magical trunk read:

HOME OR BUST!

To: Ballet Busters at Dancing Doorways Academy, United States of America

From: Imperial Theatre School, St. Petersburg, Russia, 1892.

"Leave your keys on Miss Sophia's desk," said Luis. Clang! Clink! The metal keys hit the wooden desk.

Julie felt her neck. "Oh, I can't take this home." She reached behind and unfastened the amber necklace from Tasha. She gave it a small kiss and placed it on the mantle above the fireplace.

Julie's eyes were pools of sadness. She needed Ginger to lick her face.

There was a quick knock at the door, and Tasha and her parents entered. "We came to wish you a safe trip!" said her father.

"You were all stars last night," added her mother. "We were proud of all of you. Marti, I heard they had to sew you into your costume!"

"The costume mistress took her scissors and cut me out afterwards," I said.

Tasha gave Julie a hug.

"We're so glad you came to say goodbye," said Miss Sophia.

"It's strange," said her father, "but some of the people who saw *The Nutcracker*, didn't like it."

"Why?" asked Miss Sophia.

"In the first act," said her father, "they thought there were too many children running around the stage being bad. Then they had to wait a long time to see the Sugar Plum Fairy dance with the Cavalier."

"But everyone loved the music," said Tasha.

Miss Sophia smiled. "We'll see your picture in the photos in the dance books."

"Maybe I'll meet you sometime in the Ballet Buster Super Time Tunnel," said Tasha.

"I'd love that," Julie said. "You could jump in and join us for our next adventure!"

"We're going back to the *Sleeping Beauty* ballet," Zack said.

"What?" Miss Sophia smacked her forehead. "How did you know that? I haven't told anyone yet."

Zack shrugged his shoulders with a grin.

"Zack knows everything," said Luis.

"Da, yes," said her father. "Maybe Tasha could go on the next Ballet Buster adventure."

Tasha smiled. "Maybe I could." She turned and hugged Julie tightly. They both sniffed back tears.

Miss Sophia nodded her head once. "I just found this out," she began. "If we bring a small thing from St. Petersburg back home through the Time Tunnel, we could find that person again."

Julie's eyes got huge, like the Candy Cane hoops the dancers had jumped through in the ballet.

"What do you mean?" asked Tasha's mother. "If Julie takes something small of Tasha's, she could find her later on?"

"Exactly!" Miss Sophia nodded.

"Her necklace," I blurted out. "Julie's amber necklace. Tasha gave that to her."

"Then we could find Tasha in the tunnel next year for *Sleeping Beauty*," said Miss Sophia.

"I want to see you all again," Tasha said with a laugh.

I ran over to the top of the fireplace where Julie had left the necklace and handed it to Miss Sophia.

She held it up. "We do have one problem. This necklace will be hard to get through the tunnel. Golden amber stones have their own powers. The necklace will try to fly back to Russia and it will fight the person who wears it, like a little tiger on her neck, scratching to go back." Miss Sophia nodded three times. "Who thinks they can handle this?"

My hand shot up. Zack had his up, also. Julie slowly raised hers.

"Julie," said Miss Sophia, "you seem tired and a bit sad. You might not have the strength. The necklace could become a leash on your neck, trying to yank you back to Russia." Miss Sophia felt the silver streak in the front of her hair. "Zack, I know you're strong, but…" She looked up. "I'm going to give Marti the chance to help Julie." Miss Sophia walked towards me.

"Marti, here," she said. "Turn around and I'll fasten this necklace around your neck."

I reached up and felt the hard little stones. Tasha ran over and threw her arms around me. "I know you can do it! A Ballet Buster can fight a tiger around the neck."

Miss Sophia tapped her hand on the doorway. "I hate to say this, but it is almost time for us to leave."

Tasha and her parents gave everyone kisses on both cheeks. Tasha stopped by the door, then turned. "Ballet Busters, I'll see you next year at *Sleeping Beauty*!" She gave one last wave, then took her father's hand and walked out the door.

Miss Sophia handed Julie a cotton hankie and wiped her eyes. "You didn't want to leave the United States to come here," said Miss Sophia, "and now you don't want to go home."

Julie gave a laugh through her tears. "It's a little easier now, because I'll see Tasha again."

"We can talk about that later," said Miss Sophia. "Right now, everyone gather around the magic box on my desk." The wooden container glowed with red, green, and blue sparkles.

On top, the box's arrow pointed to the shiny star with the golden writing, Mistress Sophia Violet Wusselpoof, Press Here.

Miss Sopia rubbed her fingers and thumb in the air. After a twirl, she traced the little circle on top of the golden star.

Zing! The lid popped open. Miss Sophia had that special touch.

"Ballet Busters are you ready? We'll land on the stage at Dancing Doorways Academy. Let the magic begin!"

Miss Sophia reached inside and took out the little jeweled silver box. She lifted the lid and gathered a pinch of glitter. As she opened her arms, stars surrounded us. "Speak English again!"

Our brains switched gears. We all laughed.

Miss Sophia twirled her hand above her head. "Luis and Willow, close the magical trunk."

They picked up the lid and slammed it down. Thick black straps with buckles clicked the lid shut. We pushed the tall humming magical trunk toward the white marble fireplace.

"Zack, would you and Marti bend down and open the back panel of the fireplace?" We knelt on the brick floor and pulled off a piece of wood. I peered down into the black nothingness of the Ballet Busters Super Time Tunnel. It smelled of musty cool air, like the basement of an old house.

We uncurled our bodies and stood up. "It's sure dark down there," said Zack.

I brushed my hands together to remove the dark soot and dirt. "My fingers are tingling," I added, "like electricity."

"Something special is happening," said Miss Sophia. She stood in front of the fireplace and reached inside the little silver box. Miss Sophia grabbed a pinch of glitter, circled her hand in the air, and then threw glitter on the magical trunk.

"Open to the Ballet Busters Super Time Tunnel." There was a loud roar as the back of the fireplace grandly opened.

"One, two, three, push!" said Miss Sophia. We all shoved the magical trunk through the fire place, and whoosh, it disappeared.

Miss Sophia looked at us. "Now it's our turn." She threw the whole box into the air. Little glistening stars floated around. "Come Denise, take my hand. May your ankle heal." Tiny stars landed on her leg and foot.

"Marti, take my other hand. You've got that little amber necklace that will jump around your neck."

"I'm going to take Marti's other hand," said Julie. "I want to be next to my necklace." I felt her firm grip and knew I could fight the little tiger in this necklace, with Julie on one side and Miss Sophia on the other.

She nodded her head two times. "Ballet Busters, let's go! Goodbye Russia! Dancing Doorways Academy, here we come! One, two, three, leap!"

I bent my knees and jumped into the blackness. Wind brushed past my ears. My pony tail pulled straight above my head. I opened my eyes. A huge nutcracker whirled past.

Ouch. The amber pulled at my neck. It had a life of its own and wanted to stay in Russia. We were going so fast I could not reach up and pull it off, even if I wanted to.

The Nutcracker music zipped in my ears. Next the floating notes of *The Sleeping Beauty* trickled by. Streaks of blue, purple, and pink zapped my eyes. The necklace pulled up and dug into my ears. A baby doll zoomed past. Then the vines, thorns, and stones of Sleeping Beauty's castle. A throne whizzed by. I ducked. My hands were sore from holding onto Miss Sophia and Julie.

Suddenly, I saw light. Whack! We hit the stage floor.

29

Dancing Doorways Academy

We were back at Dancing Doorways Academy. The huge Magical Trunk loomed next to me. Ouch! I rubbed my neck and ears. Phew, the amber necklace was still on, but it was all twisted. It had dug itself into my neck.

I slowly lifted my head and looked around. Ballet Busters were hunched over on the wooden stage. My hair was a tangled mess.

"Marti, your neck is all red," said Willow. "It must feel sore."

"Oh, it's nothing." I shrugged, even though it did hurt.

I held my hands out in front. "They're really

tingly," I said.

Zack started to stand up, but when he straightened his knees, he crumbled back down.

"Don't rush it, Zack," said Miss Sophia. "I'm not standing yet. Your body has had a big shock. It needs a bit of time to get used to the 21st century."

Denise slowly straightened her leg. "Hey, my ankle doesn't hurt anymore."

Nancy rolled her eyes and let out her breath. "Of course, silly. Miss Sophia said it would heal. What did you expect?"

Miss Sophia ignored Nancy and said to Denise, "The little stars worked their magic."

Willow leaned close. "The Ballet Buster Super Time Tunnel didn't change Mean Girl Nancy."

I sneaked a smile at her. We slowly stood up and moved around, even Zack. I headed towards our magical trunk. The lid was off and Zack was already walking away with an armful of his stuff.

I grabbed my bags. I put down my things and felt for the necklace. Julie still stood on the spot where the tunnel had dumped her. "Wait Julie," I said, "I have something for you."

Julie's face lit up. She spied the amber necklace.

"Oh Marti, it made it. But it's all twisted around. It must have really dug into your skin."

"Yeah," I said. "It pulled like a tiger. The amber wanted to escape the Time Tunnel and go back to Russia. The necklace is yours."

I carefully unhooked it, grimacing.

Julie took the necklace. "Your neck looks like a squirrel chewed it."

We both laughed, while Julie popped the necklace in her ballet bag.

Just then, we heard Miss Sophia's voice. "Come here."

We all gathered by the heavy velvet green curtain at the edge of our stage.

"Ballet Busters," said Miss Sophia. "We did it!

"Next year, as Zack told all of you, we will go back in time to the *Sleeping Beauty* ballet."

We all clapped.

"And as we can see from Marti's sore neck, the amber necklace made it back through the Ballet Buster Super Time Tunnel. So, Tasha will join us for our adventure next year."

We all clapped again.

"Until then," added Miss Sophia, "ballet classes begin at Dancing Doorways Academy on Monday. I expect to see you there. Your families are here to take you home."

We were all hugging when Miss Sophia spoke again. "Zack, check the magical trunk once more. I think you might be forgetting something."

Zack let out his breath. He poked his head into the magical trunk. "Uh oh!" He pulled out his soccer ball. "I did forget something. Thanks, Miss Sophia. Come on, Luis, I can take you home."

"Bye everybody!" shouted Luis. "Great dancing, and I'll see you in a couple days. Thanks, Miss Sophia!"

"See you Monday!" she said, as both boys walked out the door.

"Bye, Miss Sophia," said the Mean Girls, as they headed towards the door, their bags slung over their shoulders.

We heard a bark. "Someone couldn't wait!" said Miss Sophia with a laugh.

Ginger burst into the room, her tail wagging with excitement. Julie knelt down for a full face licking. She laughed.

"Julie," said Miss Sophia, as she petted Ginger behind the ears, "will you take the magic amber necklace home?"

Julie stood up. "I've been thinking there may be too much power in it for me." She took the amber out of her bag. "Marti, this is your reward for fighting the necklace all the way home. Take good care of it, BFF." She placed it in my hand and gave me a hug.

"I will," I grinned and hooked it back around my neck. My rainbow shined over me.

Miss Sophia smiled. "Marti is the Keeper of the Magic Amber Necklace."

Julie hugged Miss Sophia. "Come on Ginger!" and they both ran out of the theater.

Willow walked over. "You'll take good care of that, Marti. My mom still isn't here yet. She's always late."

"She'll be here soon, I'm sure," said Miss Sophia. "Willow, I'm proud of you. You did so well as a new Ballet Buster."

A small shrill voice yelled, "Marti!" I turned and my little sister, Francesca, was running towards me. Her black curls flew. I hugged her and then noticed my mother and Abuelita in the doorway. They were waving.

"Hi, Francesca," said Miss Sophia. "You look like you grew three inches!"

"Marti, Abuelita made rice pudding for you for dinner," Francesca said, pulling on my shirt sleeve. "Let's go."

"Wait Francesca," I said, "I need my stuff."

I yanked my bags upon my shoulders.

I hugged Willow goodbye. "See you at class Monday!"

"I'm definitely doing the *Sleeping Beauty* Adventure," Willow added, "and next time, I won't be late for the Ballet Buster Super Time Tunnel."

I gave Miss Sophia a big hug. "Take good care of that necklace," she said.

Then I put my hand out to Francesca, and she grabbed it. "Your new necklace is so pretty," my little sister said.

I beamed. "Let's go home. Bye, Miss Sophia. Thanks for the best Ballet Buster adventure ever!"

Miss Sophia smiled and nodded her head just once.

Appendix

PLOT: THE FIRST *NUTCRACKER* BALLET

Miss Sophia says: There are many *Nutcracker* ballets performed around the world. Some dances and names of the characters have changed, but the ballet usually has two acts. In the first *Nutcracker*, the leading girl was Clara. Here is the story of the ballet danced in 1892.

Act I: The Stahlbaum Home

The family is preparing for Christmas Eve with a large tree and festive decorations. The party begins as guests arrive. Children dance and then receive gifts. A huge clock topped by an owl strikes eight and Drosselmeyer, Clara's godfather, arrives with four life-size dolls. These special dolls dance, and Herr Drosselmeyer takes out his toy, a nutcracker. Clara loves it, but her brother Fritz breaks it, so Herr Drosselmeyer repairs it.

The party ends, and Clara sneaks downstairs in her nightgown to check on the nutcracker in its little bed.

The clock strikes midnight, as Drosselmeyer waves his arms above the clock. Mice scurry out as the tree grows. Gingerbread soldiers arrive to fight the mice. The nutcracker grows and leads the soldiers, while doctor dolls remove the wounded. The Mouse King attempts to attack the nutcracker, and Clara throws a slipper at him.

The mice leave, and the nutcracker becomes a prince. Clara and the Nutcracker Prince walk across the stage as the snowflakes dance.

Act II: Land of the Sweets

Clara and the Nutcracker Prince arrive to meet the Sugar Plum Fairy in the Land of the Sweets. The prince tells the story of what happened, and they both sit on a throne. Sweets dance for them, including a Spanish dance called "Chocolate," an Arabian dance for coffee, the Chinese tea, and a Russian dance with candy canes. Shepherdesses dance to their flutes, while the Polichinelles skip out from under Mother Ginger's huge skirt.

After the flowers waltz, the Sugar Plum Fairy and her Cavalier present their *pas de deux*. Then, the sweets do a waltz together. The Sugar Plum Fairy gives Clara and the prince a kiss, and they fly back in a sleigh led by reindeer.

GLOSSARY

Miss Sophia's Ballet and Dance Terms

Miss Sophia says: "Ballet began in Italy and moved to France, so many of the dance terms are in French."

arabesque — (French) A pose standing on one leg with the other leg raised behind. Arms can be in front, to the side, or behind the shoulder

audition — To try out for a role or part

bourrées — (French) Tiny running steps on the balls of the feet or on point

"break a leg" — Means "good luck"

chaînés — (French)Little whipping turns done on the balls of the feet or on point

choreographer — One who makes up dance steps

choreography — The dance steps

demi plié — (French) Half bend of the knees

marking — As in "marking through the steps" Doing the dance steps with very low energy to save one's strength (usually in a rehearsal)

pas de deux — (French) A dance for two, usually a man and a woman

pirouettes — (French) Turns

premier danseur — (French) Leading male dancer. He is the Cavalier in the *The Nutcracker*.

prima ballerina — (French) Leading female dancer She is the Sugar Plum Fairy in *The Nutcracker*.

rehearse —Practice before the performance

révérence — (French) Bow at the end of a ballet class or a performance

spot — Used in turns. By staring at a spot on a wall and snapping one's head around, one gets less dizzy

understudy — A back-up person. One learns a dancer's part, so if the main dancer gets sick or injured, the back-up person goes onstage in that role.

Ballet Busters' Theater and Stage Terms

backdrop — A huge painted curtain at the back of the stage for the scenery

footlights — A row of lights at the front of the stage that shines on the performer's feet

legs for the stage — Tall, narrow curtains in the wings that hide performers entering and exiting the stage

offstage — The wings on either side of the stage

opening night — the first night a ballet is performed

prop — An item brought onstage by a performer

prop table — A backstage table that holds items that go onstage. It helps performers keep track of their props.

raked stage — Older stages sloped upwards from the audience to the back. Leaps that moved forward, or downstage, looked higher

stage manager — The person who is in charge

backstage and makes sure the dancers are ready

stagehand — a person who works backstage

trapdoor — A hole in the stage covered by a flat door. Dancers pop out of the stage or fall into the floor through these holes

wings — The space on the sides of the stage, where the performers enter and exit the stage

Ballet Busters' Russian Terms

borscht — Hot purplish soup made from beets
czar (or tzar) — Royal leader of Russia
coh — Russian for "sleep"

da — Russian for "yes"

nyet — Russian for "no"

Saint Petersburg — Capital of Russia during the time of *The Nutcracker.* Home of the czars.
samovar — A large metal pot that heats and boils water

Theatre Area — Area in St. Petersburg where the ballet dancers took classes and performed

Ballet Busters' Musical Terms

baton — A small wooden stick used by the conductor to lead the orchestra

celesta — (French) a musical instrument that looks like a small piano. It has a keyboard that plays soft bell-like tones. Peter Tchaikovsky is the first composer to use this instrument. The Sugar Plum Fairy dances to it in *The Nutcracker.*

BALLET BUSTERS' FUN FACTS!

Marti asks: Who planned the dances for the first *Nutcracker* ballet?

Miss Sophia says: Marius Petipa created the ballet steps. He was born in France in 1818 and died in 1910. He was a famous choreographer (a dance maker) who trained in France but traveled to Russia in 1847 to dance. He became a ballet master and did many famous ballets, including *The Sleeping Beauty*, *The Nutcracker*, and *Swan Lake*. He became ill during *The Nutcracker*, so Lev Ivanov stepped in.

Luis asks: Who made up the ballet steps for *The Nutcracker* after Master Petipa became ill?

Miss Sophia says: Lev Ivanov, who was called the first great Russian choreographer. He was born in Russia in 1834 and died there in 1901. He was Petipa's assistant or helper. He is famous for the snow scene, where the Snowflakes flutter across the stage in star floor patterns and circles.

Tasha asks: Who wrote the music?

Miss Sophia says: Peter Tchaikovsky composed the music for *The Nutcracker*. He was born in Russia in 1840 and died in 1893, just one year after the ballet was first performed. He never knew *The Nutcracker* would become so famous. When Tchaikovsky was young, his mother took him to the ballet, so no wonder he knew this art form would always be special. His music made the ballet steps even greater.

Willow asks: Where was *The Nutcracker* ballet first performed?

Miss Sophia says: It was first danced at the Mariinsky Theatre in St. Petersburg. The theater was named by Catherine the Great in 1783. She was the Empress of Russia and loved ballet, opera, and art. She wanted St. Petersburg to be the greatest center for the arts in Europe, so she brought famous ballet masters and dancers to Russia.

⇨

Julie asks: Did the czar of Russia see *The Nutcracker*?

Miss Sophia says: The "king" of Russia, Czar Alexander III, and his family came to the first performance of *The Nutcracker* in St. Petersburg, Russia, in December 1892. They sat in their own special section in the theater. An opera was performed first and then *The Nutcracker*. It was a very long night!

Zack asks: Where did the story of *The Nutcracker* come from?

Miss Sophia says: It is based on a German fairytale by E.T.A. Hoffmann.

Willow asks: How many people were in the ballet?

Miss Sophia says: It was a large cast. More than 200 dancers were in the first *Nutcracker*.

Nancy asks: Was the ballet a success?

Miss Sophia says: No it was not well received. People did not like little children running around and playing on the stage. They weren't used to that. They also did not want to wait until the end of the ballet to see the Sugar Plum Fairy dance.

Nancy asks: How did St. Petersburg get its name?

Miss Sophia says: The city of St. Petersburg in Russia was founded in 1703 by Peter the Great and became the capital of Russia in 1712.

Denise asks: When did the Imperial Russian Ballet begin?

Miss Sophia says: The Imperial Russian Ballet was formed around 1740 in St. Petersburg, Russia. More than 150 years later, the Imperial Ballet dancers performed in the first *Nutcracker* ballet. The company is now known as the Mariinsky Ballet and is one of the best ballet companies in the world. ⇨

Zack asks: What school trained the dancers for the first *Nutcracker*?

Miss Sophia says: They studied at the Imperial Ballet School, founded in 1738 by Empress Anna in St. Petersburg, Russia. Now known as the Vaganova Ballet Academy, it remains one of the most sought after ballet schools in the world. It was named after Agrippina Vaganova, who was born in 1879 and died in 1951. She developed a Russian ballet technique that is still taught today. The academy's huge yellow buildings have arched windows and towering columns on Theatre Street. With ballet bags slung over their shoulders, dancers pass each other on the sidewalk.

Debra DeVoe

Ballet has been Debra DeVoe's passion for as long as she can remember. She began studying ballet at seven years old and has danced ever since. As a child, she was a big fan of ballerina biographies, dance histories, and ballet stories, reading ballet books in bed until all hours of the night.

DeVoe has a MAEd from George Washington University. She has retired after teaching second grade and dance for 42 years in an independent school in Howard County, Maryland. When not busy teaching ballet, she writes about dance for children and adults.
www.dancing-doorways.com

Karel Hayes

Award-winning and *New York Times* reviewed author and illustrator Karel Hayes has written and illustrated seven books and illustrated more than 25 books, six of them with her son and fellow artist John Gorey.

Her artwork has been shown in New York City art clubs, the Cincinnati Museum of Natural History, the Philadelphia Museum of Fine Art's Sales Gallery, Surroundings Gallery in Sandwich, NH, and several galleries throughout the U. S.
www.karelhayes.com

Praise

Ballet Busters Leap into the First Nutcracker is a delightful and exciting tale of history and emotion. DeVoe weaves the history of the making of the first *Nutcracker* with the emotions of young dancers' struggles to reach their goals. Nineteenth Century Russian culture and the characters surrounding the *Nutcracker's* premiere are brought to life through the lens of twenty-first century children, ultimately illustrating how friendships are built and goals can become reality. As a former child ballerina, and now dance educator, I found *Ballet Busters Leap Into the First Nutcracker* educational, fun, and heartfelt. This book has broad appeal as it illuminates this beloved ballet while appealing to the very emotions young dancers may be grappling with. DeVoe offers insight into negotiating the emotional pathways of growing and creating meaningful relationships through an intriguing twists and turns of events keeping you on the edge of your seat while traveling through time. I recommend *Ballet Busters Leap Into the First Nutcracker* as an art educator, artist and mom. Personally, I can't wait until the next ballet book.

— *Sandra M. Perez, Associate Professor*
Dance Education, Towson University

What a delightful trip to read *Ballet Busters Leap into the First Nutcracker* by Debra DeVoe, my first dance teacher in Columbia, Maryland. The description of the first Nutcracker classical ballet, and especially Theatre Street in St. Petersburg, was accurate and charming. It made me want to return to the city where ballet continues to thrive. It certainly brought back thoughts on just how wonderful it is to be reminded of young dancers and their adventures.

—Michele Kelemen, National Public Radio Diplomatic Correspondent

This story has it all! Intrigue, suspense, beautiful imagery, history, and time travel. A perfect novel for any second or third grader. DeVoe's ability to gender-neutralize the oft female-driven ballet landscape is a rare treat.

—Angela J. Horjus, School Librarian, Glenelg Country School

Tremendous story that takes you back in time! I recommend that all kids read this, especially those who take ballet. Educational, creative, and captivating.

—Svetlana Kravtsova, Founding Artistic Director, L'Etoile, the Russian Ballet Academy of Maryland

Notes

Made in the USA
Monee, IL
05 November 2020

46782775R00142